W9-AXH-954

DISCARD

The Family

LANELLE DICKINSON KEARNEY

A Sequel to The Farm

CAPPER PRESS
Topeka, Kansas

Copyright © 1984 By LaNelle Dickinson Kearney
All rights reserved.
No part of this book may be used or reproduced in any manner
whatsoever without written permission except in the case of brief
quotations embodied in critical articles and reviews.

All characters and incidents in this book are fictitious. Any
resemblance to actual people or events is purely coincidental.

Published by Capper Press
616 Jefferson, Topeka, Kansas 66607

Cover Illustration and Calligraphy: *Catherine Seibel-Ledeker*
Production Manager: *Diana J. Edwardson*
Editor: *Michele R. Webb*
Proofreader: *Tammy R. Dodson*

ISBN 0-941678-30-X
First printing, October 1991
Printed and bound in the United States of America

*The Family was first published as a serialized novel in Capper's magazine
(formerly Capper's Weekly) from
June 5, 1984, through October 9, 1984.*

For more information about Capper Press titles
or to place an order, please call:
(Toll-free) 1-800-777-7171, extension 107, or (913) 295-1107.

Capper Fireside Library

*F*eaturing
the most popular novels previously
published in *Capper's* magazine, as well as
original novels by favorite *Capper's* authors, the
Capper Fireside Library presents the best of fiction in
quality softcover editions for the family library. Born out of
the great popularity of *Capper's* serialized fiction, this
series is for readers of all ages who love a good
story. So curl up in a comfortable chair,
flip the page, and let the storyteller
whisk you away into the world
of this novel from the
*Capper Fireside
Library.*

Hunter 3-93 6.99 103 P.

Dedicated to Mama, to Jean,
and to Papa, who had such blue eyes.

Contents

The Family

CHAPTER ONE

Calvin

*I*t was 1924. Calvin O'Neil had reached the age of ninety-two in very good grace, the past mingling healthily with the present. Often times now his mind recalled the day when he had been ninety. Nothing special had occurred, but the family had rallied around him in an unusually merry mood, respecting his wish that no outsiders be invited, and they had had a family picture made.

Two years ago I was ninety, he thought, and I was surprised that I had lived so long. Now here I am ninety-two and past. When does it stop?

At that moment a tiny, shriveled eighty-three-year-old woman silently entered the room and took the companion chair opposite her husband's. Calvin had often teased her about struggling to pin her three hairs up on her head, and on this cold day, hair and head were covered by a warm, lace-decorated cap.

"Nan," Calvin said. "Can you remember my birthday party when I was ninety?"

"Of course, I can. I can remember my own birthday parties, too. And I recall the party we gave Tinette, too, soon after her marriage to Earl. Now let me nap." Mrs. O'Neil pulled her dark wool wrapper around the gray dress she was wearing, and rested her head on the back of her wing-back chair.

"Earl," Calvin said aloud. Then he, too, leaned back in his big chair and thought a little about Earl Norris, how long the man had been part of a family that never really wanted him. The old man let his mind talk steadily to himself, underneath the tight white curls that gave him such a distinctive, yet jaunty look.

There was Tinette, head over heels in love with one man, followed constantly by another, that ape Walton, and making up her mind to marry a third, Earl Norris. He was after her all the time, too, but I never thought she'd take him. There'd not been much love in that room upstairs — but still there'd been lots of offspring. Tinette's youngest, Wanda, a corker if there ever was one, was a hard nut to crack. The others, Ted, Sara, and Franklin, they didn't mean a lot to Wanda. Sometimes I wonder if a few hard licks would have taken out some of her sassy ways, but neither she nor any of the others had ever got any. Sometimes she is sweet, though, not sweet like Priscilla, but just kinda nice. It was a good day when Ted married sweet Priscilla, and a better day yet when little Marguerite had been born.

At that point Calvin remembered that it was time for him to move out into the sitting room to see that happy first-grader as she got home from school. "But what had I been thinking of?" he asked himself. As he reached with his gnarled left hand to steady himself against the stand table, he noticed the large family picture that had been taken on his ninetieth birthday. "Now I remember," he whispered to himself, "that picture showed me. I was wanting to think about my party when only the family was present."

The old man stood upright and took the picture in his hands. Scrutinizing it for perhaps the five hundredth time he saw the saucy Wanda seated on the arm of her father's chair with one slim hand on Earl's shoulder. Calvin wondered if she would taint lives as Earl Norris had done. Then his gaze took in himself and Tinette, and little

Marguerite seated between them. Priscilla stood behind the sofa. "Odd how much she resembles Tinette, her mother-in-law," he mused. Franklin and Sara stood side by side, and Ted knelt beside his grandmother's chair. There we are, he thought. Me and old Nan. Tinette and her four. Two in-laws, though Priscilla seems like our own, and one great-grandchild.

The day that picture was taken had been one of Calvin's best days, and nobody wanted it to end, not even the restless Wanda. But it had ended and Calvin often looked at the picture with something like wistful wonderment. All of those people from tiny Nancy. And from stalwart Tinette.

Sometimes he thought of his daughter's sadness in losing her real love. That person had been treacherous, fostering love in Tinette when he knew that he was not free to marry her. As the years had passed, over thirty of them, Calvin had become so embittered over it that he couldn't trust himself to think of it. Turning his thoughts to Earl Norris didn't give much happy relief either, but in the last fifteen or more years, the man had given many hours of congenial companionship. "We must be fair," Calvin would say to Nancy. "Earl has straightened out." To this, Nancy once had replied that to straighten out was the only possible posture left for him.

Calvin replaced the family picture onto the stand and slowly walked back to the sitting room. Suddenly it seemed that life had cut in on his habit of reminiscing. He had inadvertently overheard the words "Weston O'Neil," spoken by his grandson. The intake and effect of these words changed Calvin's life. Closed it.

When in her late teens, Tinette O'Neil had met Earl Norris, erstwhile dentist. He had pressed his attentions on her, as had the wily Bill Walton. Walton had at that time acquired land which Calvin had coveted, and needed as an outlet to the highway ever since he had taken a homestead claim in 1863. Tinette was not entirely comfortable around Earl, but the rude tactics that Walton used in his efforts to woo her practically pushed her towards Earl.

Then when Tinette had met her true love and found that he already had a wife, she quite literally escaped Walton's advances by marrying Earl Norris. Tinette was not the only one who had fallen in love with Weston O'Neil. Her parents had wanted to take this distant cousin into their home as a son. Now for over thirty years, his name had never been spoken aloud.

Quite by accident, the old man had learned that Walton was at last ready to sell the desired property, and to a man named Weston O'Neil. Calvin had risen to his feet on the cold February day and bade his grandson drive him to Walton's place. He went into the dilapidated old house by himself, and there he disclosed to Walton the secret of Tinette's love and her life of sacrifice. Bill Walton, having carried his true love for Tinette all of those years, now felt akin to her as never before. In an impromptu decision, he yielded the deed to Calvin, and promised to sell the rest of his property to the man who had been bidding against Weston O'Neil. Bill was leaving immediately for a place in California.

That evening at supper Calvin told the family he had acquired the long desired piece of property. He said he had put it, along with the farm itself, in Ted's name. That night as he lowered his body onto his bed, he thought, "Tomorrow I shall give attention to — "

Quite before midnight, Nancy awoke from her sleep. Something seemed different. She lay very still and listened. What she was listening for was not to be heard. She had been a wakeful sleeper beside her husband all of their sixty-one years together and always when she would lie awake, Calvin's steady breathing would rise as a comfort to her, an assurance of protection against too much sadness, against illness, and against a dreaded loneliness. Now there was no sound. The assurance was gone.

Calvin O'Neil's body reposed between the front parlor windows. Tinette had drawn back both of the long ecru drapes to let as much light as possible fill the room. As she glanced out, she noticed the hearse that had carried her father back home had just turned out of the driveway to head back to town. She thought, "Tomorrow you will be coming back. To take him from me. To put him where I shall never be able to see him again."

The heavy-set woman turned from the windows and sank into a chair which had been pushed away from its usual place to allow the men to move the bier. It was a chair of deep blue velvet brocade, one that matched the long sofa and two other chairs. Tinette had selected the set, plus an extra chair of cream-colored velvet brocade, but Calvin had paid for the purchase. He referred to it as "Tinette's parlor suit."

Leaning her head against the chair back, she whispered quitely to herself. "Papa," she whispered, "what do I do now? I've never been away from you one day in all my life." It was true. Almost true. Even counting the few nights in her girlhood when she had stayed in town with friends, she had never been away from him really. It seemed to her now that she had always been wanting to hurry back home. Even her first and every married night was spent in her father's house. Soon he would be gone.

Wanting to see him again, Tinette rose and tiptoed over the soft, rosy carpet to stand beside the lifeless form. He still looked handsome, still looked strong (at least his face had that appearance). She touched his white curls, so tight to his head, and the touch was too much. She cried freely and thought, "I touch your curls, but what I long for is to see your blue eyes again."

Ted broke in upon her reverie. "Mother, shall I bring Grandmother in now to see Grandfather?"

"Have you looked at him yet, Ted?"

"Not exactly, Mom," her son answered softly.

"Come see how fine he looks."

"Mother, let me see him when I bring Grandmother in."

Ted Norris turned and left the room, leaving his mother to grieve alone. She removed a handkerchief from a pocket of her cover-all apron, a pale pink handkerchief smelling of lavender, and tried to wipe her cheeks dry. But fresh tears fell. Touching her father's cold hands shocked her tears into abating for the moment, and she hurriedly left the room. She took no notice whether anyone was in the sitting room or kitchen, and hastily grabbed her heavy everyday coat and head shawl from a hook on the milk porch. Stopping only long enough to don the coat and to throw the shawl over her head, she swiftly walked out into the area that Calvin had always called "Nan's side yard."

To the immediate left of the house was a cave which the old people had fixed up in their pioneer days. The mound over it was covered with a thin coating of frost, and the handle by which she opened the door (it was horizontal to the ground and could be fastened back with a huge iron hook) was icy cold. Tinette was stout but her slender legs carried her rapidly down the eight steps and into the food-filled cave. She leaned her head against a shelf full of canned fruit, the heavy shawl protecting her forehead from the wooden edge, and let loose all the sobs that were inside her. Having lost her power to cry any more, at last she sat down on a keg and tried to think about what her life would be like without her father.

When Tinette had hurriedly left the parlor she had not noticed that Ted was still lingering in the hall. He stood at the front door, looking at life to come, as it were, through the haze of the curtain. He saw his grandad's pheasants as they pecked away at next-to-nothing near their shelter on the other side of the fence that separated the "little pasture," as Calvin had dubbed it, from the driveway. Grandfather's pheasants, some brown, some brightly arrayed, but no Grandfather. He looked further, a bit to the left, and where the ground began to slope off he saw Grandfather's beautiful grove of cottonwoods. Trees, but no Grandfather. "I can't seem to bring him to mind," Ted thought. And he screamed mentally, "I can't see Grandfather!"

Ted's father was descending the stairs, and with him was Ted's eighteen-year-old sister, Wanda. Wanda was dressed in a gray, short box-pleated wool skirt that flared out as she took each downward step, revealing more of her fine, slim legs that were replicas of her mother's. Over a white shirt was a red flannel vest. It fastened with one large, gray button at her waist, and as she crossed the hall to the parlor door, Ted turned and noticed that her fingers kept undoing the button, then putting it back through the buttonhole.

Wordlessly, Earl and Wanda walked to the coffin. Wordlessly, they looked at the grand old man. Wordlessly, they left the room. Earl Norris turned towards the sitting room door and passed through it on his way to the kitchen. The huge blue coffeepot, full and giving out a full aroma, was at-the-ready on Tinette's big, black range. The fellow was feeling sorry for himself and he looked at the coffee as a bit of comfort. His usual cup was not in its place and Earl took it as a planned offense against him. An old mug-style cup was standing on the warmer, and he poured it full. Walking over to a south window, he held the mug in his hand for a while. His gaze was upon it, and he felt his left hand rattling change in his trouser pocket without really knowing he was doing it.

Calvin O'Neil, he thought. I married his daughter and what did I ever get for it? Wanda, I guess. At least maybe I got Wanda. But the old man had all the rest. Now he is gone. I meant nothing to him and he meant nothing to me. But the others, they fitted in tight. Tight together. Now their glue is gone, and I wonder how tight they'll fit together now.

Earl raised the mug to his lips and immediately spat out the small swallow he had taken. He had not noticed that someone else had used the cup for sweetened coffee, and some of the sugar had remained to spoil his drink. As he was still feeling sorry for himself, the dirty mug really made him feel put upon. As if for spite, or just to show the world that he did not care, he drank the entire mugful and strode fussily back upstairs to his bedroom.

Wanda, in leaving the parlor, had ignored the presence of her brother in front of the outside door, and had merely gone behind him and on upstairs to her room. Her thoughts were strange for the occasion because they did not contain an expression of grief or loss. To her, Grandad was gone. Everyone had known he could not last forever, and he had not been much good to anyone for a long time. She would be glad when they had had the funeral and everything would get back to normal.

When Wanda opened the door to the bedroom, she heard sounds of sniffling. As she actually entered the room, she heard crying. Her sister was seated on the edge of the bed, holding a white handkerchief to her reddened nose. She had on an old-fashioned looking black dress, and Wanda wondered where in the world she could have dug it up.

"Oh, Wanda," said Sara between sobs, "how can we let him go?"

"It is not ours to 'let' him go or stay, Sara."

"Nothing will be the same without Grandfather. Nothing."

"You mean we won't be living here anymore?"

"Why, Wanda. What in the world do you mean? Of course, we will all go on living here. This is our home."

"You mean then that you won't be working for Franklin anymore?"

"Wanda! What can you be saying? Of course, I'll be working as usual."

"Then what do you mean when you say that nothing will be the same?"

This was too much for Sara. She wanted to tell Wanda that in all of her thirty-one years she had never heard of such callousness, but she felt that her tears were coming too hard now for her to speak. She went out into the hall and down the stairs to stand beside her two brothers. Franklin had joined Ted, and Sara slipped between them for a moment.

"Have you been in yet?" asked Franklin. Negative shakes from the other two heads. "I am going in now," he said and as he turned to leave, his sister also turned and they walked into the parlor together. Each looked at the grandfather a moment, then at one another.

"Sad," said Franklin, and his sister nodded, wiping her tears away. "Sara, do you think any of Mom's jam cake is still on the sideboard?" She nodded and they went into the dining room.

Out in the hall, Ted Norris was beginning to feel cold. In spite of all precautions to make the front door airtight, wind from the north did creep in. He rubbed his hands together, took one very deep breath, and entered his grandparents' room, at the foot of the stairs, just opposite the parlor. Nancy Hawkins O'Neil looked lifeless as she sat in her big chair, just staring at the empty chair across from her.

"Grandmother?"

"Ted, sit down. Sit down there in front of me."

"In Grandfather's chair?"

"Yes. He would never want it to remain empty. He would want the Chief to sit in it, close by me. It was comical how he would call you 'Chief.' Made me think he had a kind thought of old Black Thunder after all."

"Did he call me 'Chief,' Grandmother?"

"You never heard him? Well, I'll swan. When I would mention the old warrior now and then, mostly of late years I took to recallin' him, Cal would say, 'Ted's a chief, too.' "

"Grandmother, you and Grandfather have made life wonderful for me."

"And your Mom. She has made it wonderful for you, too."

"Oh, of course! Mother, of a certainty. But behind her, always you and Grandfather."

"Where is Priscilla?"

"She took Marguerite up to the Katchalls until after the funeral is over. Then she is going to show Marguerite the grave and explain how it is."

Nancy had put on a dress that was a favorite of Calvin, a dark brown velvet that reached her ankles. At the neck was a collar of heavy cream-colored lace, and several large velvet-covered buttons closed the dress. She was so thin that her skin was like parchment, and the hands she held out to her grandson looked like sticks of bamboo. Ted lifted her to her feet and gave her a gentle hug, holding back on the love he really wanted her to feel because of her frail frame.

It was their turn to pay their respects to all that was

left, to the body that so recently ensconced such a vibrant spirit. They looked for a while upon his visage, Nancy patted and fretted a bit with the gray suit, and Ted tried to blink back his tears.

After a while Nancy sat down on the far end of the long sofa, and told Ted that she wanted to remain there. When he had left the room, the eighty-three-year-old woman spoke, "You left me, Cal. I told you never to do that. I didn't think you would."

Maybe half an hour passed before she spoke again, this time to say, "You never should have done it. This is your place to be. Why did you leave it?"

Tears came and Nancy drew a lace-edged 'kerchief from a little pocket that Tinette had thoughtfully sewn on the dress. She covered her tiny face with the white linen cloth and she wept. Later she recovered, saying, "I forgive you, Cal. I know you could not help leaving me. You were always so good to me."

All day long Nancy kept vigil, sitting on the sofa, silently observing mourners come and go. Her only response to any of them was to give a little flutter of the lace-edged 'kerchief.

Ted left the room, wishing keenly for Priscilla. But in the kitchen sat his two pals, the remaining two of his trilogy. The three then stood together, arms around one another, and they wept. Never, never would they forget the man who had been father and grandfather to them.

The funeral was held at the Episcopal Church and burial followed at the town cemetery. The church had been full to overflowing and every person went over to the cemetery. Many of the people were crowded into cars, some rode in carriages, and many just walked the few blocks. But all of them were at the gravesite, and all crowded around to see Ted Norris toss the traditional handful of dirt onto the lowering casket. Seeing it go down, slowly down and down, was a cruel sight.

All of the Norris family, Nancy O'Neil, friends and more friends wept freely. Tinette and her two daughters stepped to the side of the grave and each let one flower fall onto the casket.

The crowd stayed on, visiting with one another and sharing memories that concerned the last days of the late Calvin O'Neil. It would be impossible to forget him, they felt. If it had not been for the big crowd that surrounded the family, what then occurred could never have happened. Tinette stooped down to tuck her mother's neck-scarf into the coat more firmly, and as she did so she glanced through a gap in the crowd and saw a man who was retrieving a glove from the ground. She stood. All she could see was the immediate circle. Then she saw him again. He had made a place for himself and was beckoning her to pass around the group and come to him.

Weston O'Neil would never have been brave enough to enter the group and publicly face Tinette, even though she and her mother were the only persons there who knew the man. Bill Walton would not have recognized him since their only contact had been by mail. But to stand outside the circle and wait for Tinette to get a chance to go to him, that was something he could do. Gradually she was able to ease her way out from the family circle, and the group of mourners quickly closed ranks to get closer to the most bereaved.

The sight of Weston O'Neil did nothing to Tinette except make her long even more for her father. Oddly enough, the staunch Tinette spoke exactly as her wailing mother had done sixty years before. "Why, oh, why," Tinette whispered to herself, "why did my father have to leave me to face this day?"

There was no handshake, no smile, no word of greeting for Weston. She looked him straight in the eye, looked right into his big, blue O'Neil eyes, and said, "Weston, why are you here? You must know that Walton let the property go to someone else. He has already taken his leave of this town. Now you must do the same."

"No, Tinette, no."

"The sight of you would finish off my poor old mother whose heart you broke years ago."

"I have to talk to you."

"Weston O'Neil, turn and get out of here. Leave before this crowd breaks and my family gets a look of you."

"Tinette, I am ill. My heart, I was told, cannot last much longer. My son — "

"Your son?"

"My wife found me eventually. She died giving birth. She was too old, you see."

"You have a son?"

"Loy is now nearing sixteen. That is why I wanted the property. No, Tinette, Walton did not sell to someone else."

"Papa himself got part of it."

"I got the rest."

"Weston O'Neil, get out. Leave at once!"

"Tinette, promise me that when I am gone you will let Loy live on that property where you can sort of look after him some. Maybe even help him get on."

The man grabbed her arms and Tinette feared that at any moment his presence would become known to her unsuspecting family. She was strong and he was weak, but she could not shake his grip from her arms.

"Promise, Tinette. He is all I have, and he has no one."

"I shall do as you say if you leave immediately and never return, and if the boy stays away as long as you live."

Weston O'Neil dropped his hand and walked away. After a few steps he stopped and faced her once more.

"Thank you," he said.

His car was the first to leave the cemetery.

Somehow Tinette O'Neil got through the day. Priscilla had returned, having stopped at the cemetery to show Marguerite all the flowers that banked Calvin's grave. In her quiet and understanding way, Priscilla had been able to get through in an acceptable way to the six-year-old. She explained about the transfer from Earth to Heaven, making it clear that it was a nice thing that happened to everyone. She described the fact of loneliness that the family would endure, assuring that tears would be a natural way to ease the loneliness. She had disclosed her own feelings of sadness when her grandparents had made the Big Journey, and even told the child that Grandfather's departure was giving her intense pain. Lastly, she told of the love and respect that the dead man had built up among the townspeople and farmers. To endorse this, she stopped the old Chevrolet at the cemetery so Marguerite could see the huge offering of flowers.

Their arrival at the O'Neil farm eased Tinette a great deal. Marguerite did not say much but she sat on her dear grandmother's lap for a long while. Even when she finally wandered outside, she merely sat quietly in her swing. Calvin had hung a new swing for her. Above her were the wide branches of the tall pine tree. In her grandmother's arms and under the pine branches she had a feeling that everything would be all right.

Priscilla took over the work, setting out food for the family and friends, food largely carried in by sympathetic friends. Jim Stanton from across the road saw that Marguerite seemed bewildered and he asked permission to take the little girl home with him. He had twin lambs that she could hold and feed with a bottle. Jim, Tinette's age, had married very early, a couple of years even before she did, and his wife, Flora, was helping Priscilla.

There was far more food than the seven members of the O'Neil-Norris group could eat, so it was a good thing that thoughtful friends dropped in to "sit down" with them. At noon and again at six o'clock, a dozen or more friends came to share the food. Their presence made it easier for the family to take food. Reminiscences were forthcoming, many of them bringing chuckles, because Calvin O'Neil's wit was one of his charms. They recalled when some visitor from the East had been taken out to see the yellow bank of roses beneath Calvin's spreading pine tree. It had been hot summer time but the visitor asked about winter temperatures. Calvin told him how very cold it could get, and added that it once got so cold that ice formed and pushed out of holes until it stood up like fence posts. "And the feller believed Cal," one neighbor said and everyone shouted with laughter.

Some friends dropped by for an hour or two between and after eating times. For them there was pie (seventeen pies had been brought in), cake of every kind, and always plenty of coffee. Nancy sat in the parlor at one end of the long sofa and admonished Flora and Priscilla to keep pots of coffee hot and ready. "Strong, real coffee. Not coffee essence that Cal and I had to use in the early days."

The two women worked until nearly midnight, slicing the hams and roasts and the baked hens, keeping big trays of sandwiches standing on the sideboard. Some walked around munching a sandwich. Others wandered into the dining room and sat down at the large, oval, oak table. The last thing that little Marguerite remembered that evening was sitting on her daddy's lap at the table and hearing Flora Stanton's mother eat cheese. Each time she took a bite, her false teeth loosened and gave an annoying click. Then the child fell asleep and was carried up to bed. It had been a difficult two days for everyone, but the presence of well-loved friends saw the family through them.

CHAPTER TWO

Nancy

*T*he governor of the household, the check, the rein, was gone. The glue that held it together was no more.

It would be difficult to say which person noticed it most keenly, felt it most deeply. Most of the family went about with a sick feeling for months after the break. There was not one of them who did not feel a loosening of the strings that had held them all more or less tightly to a stalwart way of life. Not a religious way of life necessarily, but a dutiful way. All of the family touched base from time to time at St. Mark's, but regular attendance had actually been observed only by Priscilla, and that in the interest of proper training for her daughter. Tinette herself had let lax habits creep into her spiritual life ever since her children had been small.

But Calvin O'Neil had somehow or other, with little direct teaching, been able to get across the idea of strong backbone, elbow grease, no excuses; do your job, never put off that which must be done now — all these aspects of his way of life had dominated every member of his family. True, one of the in-laws found this to be such an impossible blueprint to follow that he avoided others' stares and his own sense of guilt by retreating to his own room for most of the day. And true, one of this man's daughters for the most part had adopted a devil-may-care attitude towards the work ethic. Yet even she found it impossible to shirk very much on school work that was her responsibility.

16

Calvin had made an impact. While he lived, no one questioned his way of looking at life. He had thought life was Duty, and no one disputed. But at his departure, the ropes which had bound the family members to Duty definitely loosened.

Why was this so? For one thing, their spirits were dampened. When the grand gentleman died, he left behind cracks in the hearts of his family. Not all of them realized it at once, or even at the same time, but every one of them began to tell time by "When Grandfather died," "After Grandfather left," "While Grandfather was alive," and "Until Grandfather was taken."

For another thing, nearly one hundred years had passed since Calvin's birth, and a different century was upon the lives of his progeny. They now lived in a lighter age: Dresses were shortened (along with ladies' hair), dance styles fostered a permissive closeness, risque slang entered the language, women were given privileged rights, the last war that was ever to be had brought peace and prosperity. Those who had toiled so hard now had given over to the enjoy-it age.

Calvin O'Neil had belonged to the Modern Woodmen group, Nancy and Tinette to Royal Neighbors. Each one of the three had a substantial insurance policy in one of two groups, but none of them had entered into the social part. Often urged to attend certain lodge functions, on rare occasions they had "gone in" for supper. But the O'Neil-Norris clan seemed to find itself adequate in most respects. They met their neighbors and friends at fairs and at holiday celebrations, funerals and weddings, and occasional church "doings." But as a rule their associates had been themselves. Even their only in-law, so far that is, had come from the family's closest friends.

There was a restlessness abroad in the land and it seemed to reach the O'Neil farm about the time of Calvin's death. Even though only one male O'Neil had ever lived on the place, and three Norris men, it was always known as the O'Neil farm. Ted Norris owned it outright, even before Calvin's death. It was still the O'Neil farm.

At about the turn of the century, Julius Katchall had persuaded Calvin to buy some river property close to his own. The two men went in together for some of the land and Calvin purchased more by himself. Katchall had soon died, his wife having preceded him, and Calvin later sold his half to Priscilla's father. Then as the century drew to a close, Calvin leased the other property to a fellow who hauled sand out of it. This brought good income to Calvin and also a good price when he sold it in 1920.

When Grandfather O'Neil died, he left the money from the two property sales, along with the interest money, to his four grandchildren with Wanda's part remaining in trust until she reached her majority. Tinette was named as the beneficiary on her father's main insurance policy, and Marguerite on a smaller one. It was almost phenomenal, strange and unusual to be sure, but not one of the family questioned the fact that Ted received not only the farm, but an equal amount of money as his siblings. Subconsciously, each one seemed to take it as just because Ted was the oldest and the one who had worked on the land. For twenty years, ever since he was twelve, he had helped his grandfather work and improve the farm. It belonged to him.

The first year in which Calvin had begun to make a profit was 1871, the year Tinette was born. That year he took one hundred dollars and put it in the bank under the name of Nancy H. O'Neil. From that year until his death, he never missed depositing a sum in that account. The amount varied. For several years it was up to five hundred dollars, and for two years he had been able to put in ten times that amount for her.

Nancy held the bankbook herself, and she thought no one knew about it. She smiled whenever she saw her bankbook in the small handkerchief drawer, one of two little drawers on the top of her black walnut chiffonier. In the other drawer were some smelling salts and a flat box of pink pills she occasionally needed for indigestion.

One day when Wanda was in her fourteenth year, Nancy had needed her smelling salts while she was seated at the kitchen table. The girl had run to get them, and upon opening the wrong drawer had seen the bankbook. Nancy H. O'Neil, the cover read. Wanda glanced through it and later told the news to the rest of the family after Nancy had turned to her bed.

"Guess who is rich? Gran is. Gran is rich!"

"You mean Granmama?" Sara asked prissily.

"You know who I mean, Sara."

"Well! 'Gran' is not a proper name for our grandmother."

"Oh, Sara," Ted began.

"Well, I don't care, Ted. It sounds cut-off. And that is disrespectful."

"Wanda, tell us what you were saying," Franklin said.

"I saw Gran's passbook."

"Where?"

"In the pill drawer. Or the other one."

"Well?"

"It said 'Nancy H. O'Neil' on it, and inside are pages of figures. Gran is rich!"

Ted nodded his head slowly. "Now I look back and recall something about that."

"What was it?"

"Well, Grandfather once or twice went to get a passbook from Grandmother before I took him to the bank. I never thought what it was or anything, and I never went into the bank with him."

Franklin shook his head in wonderment. "He had an account for Grandma. Did you know that, Mom?"

"I think so," was all that Tinette said, but in this way the rest of the family gained knowledge that Nancy had her own money.

One day after the funeral, before Nancy had time to join the family for supper, Franklin asked his mother if their grandmother still had her bank account.

"I think so," Tinette whispered as her mother entered the room.

Part of each day Nancy O'Neil would go into the parlor to sit, a ritual she had never performed before her husband's death. There was no fireplace in the "new" sections of the house, that is, in the front two rooms downstairs or in any room upstairs. Ted had always entered his grandparents' room early to bring the fire alive and see that the room was warm enough. It had a large coal stove as did the room across the hall.

The day after the funeral, and for several more days, Nancy asked Ted to light the stove in the parlor, too. After that he did not have to be told, but always saw to both fires.

And the day after the funeral, Tinette went as usual to help her mother dress. Nancy had a big surprise for her daughter. She was already fully dressed. Nancy had put on the brown velvet dress and had even laced her shoes. True, Ted had to tie them a little later, but she had been able to get them on and laced reasonably well.

"Bring my coffee to the parlor, Tinette. I'll be out for my breakfast later."

From then on, the tiny old lady dressed herself and crossed over to the parlor to sit at one end of the long sofa where she had last viewed the body of her departed man. It was after eight o'clock when she awakened, and by then the room would be fairly warm and fairly light because

20

Tinette would have been in to pull back the drapes.

By Sunday Nancy had been into the new habit for five days, the funeral having been on Wednesday. Still wearing her brown velvet dress she felt dressed up enough to receive the few callers who came to see how everyone was getting along. Flora Stanton had come every day, but on Sunday Jim came with her. They were ready to go to the Christian Church for Sunday School.

Jim stepped into the parlor. "Mrs. O'Neil you look pert." He pronounced it "peert," the way Calvin had always said it.

"Jim boy," she answered, "I have something here that I want Flora to have."

"Well now, Mrs. O'Neil, that's a kind thing to do fer my missis."

Nancy reached into her little pocket and pulled out a handkerchief of white lawn, edged in blue tatting. She laid it on her lap and slowly unfolded it to bring to view a beautiful pin. It was a gold brooch from which shone a bright emerald. Pearls encircled the gem. She lifted it carefully and handed it to Jim Stanton.

"For Flora," she said. "Well, really for you, Jim."

The man took the lovely pin into his own rough hand and looked at it admiringly. "I've seen you wear this, haven't I?"

"Maybe you have. Not often. Do you know where that came from?" The man shook his head and Nancy continued. "When Tinette was two, and you were about the same age, of course, we had a gathering here. Cal and I had been married ten years and friends brought presents. Your brother Sam was here, naturally. He was the best man that ever lived. He took care of you boys just like an old mother hen. We never got to meet your folks, being killed as they were before you all moved in over there, but this pin had been given by someone way back there to your mother. Sam gave it to me. It's yours."

"But Mrs. O'Neil, this has been yours fer more than fifty years."

"It's yours. For Flora. She's such as good woman."

"What about Tinette?"

"She's good, too," said Nancy, laughing at her little joke.

"But I mean, shouldn't Tinette have it?"

"No, this is yours. For Flora. It's all you have that was ever part of your mother."

"Then I'll say thank you, but it don't seem right."

"It's right. I'll tell you, Jim, when Flora gets tired of it, after Ted's baby is a woman, maybe you'll let Marguerite have it."

Jim Stanton's troubled expression changed to one of relief, and smilingly he nodded and thanked Nancy again for the gift. When he went into the kitchen he showed it to Flora.

"Take it, Flora. Mrs. O'Neil wants you to have it."

Tinette stepped forward and took the pin from Jim's hand. She let Flora admire it for a moment, then pinned it to the woman's black silk waist.

"Mrs. O'Neil says that it came from my own mother, Flora."

"It did." Tinette told them. "It was among your mother's things and was hers."

"What is that stone, Tinette?"

"Why, it's an emerald! A jewel that queens wear. An emerald set in gold with pearls for a wreath."

"Is it all right for me to have it?"

"Of course, it is, Flora. That pin belonged to Jim's own mother."

"But Tinette, haven't I seen your mother wear it?"

"Perhaps you have, Flora. But Mother gave it back to Jim. He wants you to wear it. It is your brooch now."

"Jim," Flora said emotionally. "I'll have to go to church every Sunday now so as to wear the brooch." She suddenly thought of the old woman who had saved it and passed it along and off she went to proffer her thanks.

As the days passed, Nancy traded the brown velvet dress for her dark blue wool, and again for a warm gray dress. One week she even dressed in a black silk suit complete with a cream-colored blouse. The family had never seen her wear that suit at home and rarely anywhere. Formerly it had to be a very special occasion before Nancy would wear her good silk suit.

One day she spilled coffee on the jabot which decorated the blouse. She wiped it with her napkin but the stain remained. When she walked back to the kitchen for her breakfast, she bade Tinette to get busy and make another waist or two with which to trade off.

"A yellow one, Tinette. And one in pink," she said. "Phone Sara up at the store and tell her to bring some goods home. Some nice Crepe de Chine."

It was a new role for the old pioneer. The fact of Nancy leaving her bedroom early enough to have coffee carried to her in the parlor was enough of an innovation to startle the family. Then to see her in some of her very best "going-a-visitin' " togs gave them further shock. But to hear her voice with a positive sound, with even a tone of command in it, was to puzzle the descendants who had been thinking of their grandmother as "about done for."

From the day of Calvin's death until her own, Nancy never again dressed in any apparel but the best. Wools and silks and velvets most of the year, with fine lawns, pongees, tubsilks and tissue gingham for the hot months. Toward the end of her long life, these materials were made up into peignoirs, robes and wrap-arounds, made for her ease in putting them on.

When the fact of her "wealth," relative though it was, became undisputable knowledge, it awarded her a place of right in which she could dress as she pleased and sit where she liked without being challenged.

Of course, she did not sit in the parlor all day long. She took every meal with the family in the kitchen, or on Sundays and special occasions in the dining room. Sometimes she would go up the stairs all by herself. She would walk into and through each of the four rooms, even when Earl was at his desk writing, at what she did not know and did not care.

At the end of the hall she would go into the bathroom that Calvin had "seen to." She liked the gleam of it, so white and clean.

At the top of the stairs, contemplating the descent she would balk.

"Priscilla," she would call, "come here."

Then someone would hear her and go to help her slowly down the steps, two feet placed on each one before tackling the next one. Sometimes Earl would be watching for her, and he would step out into the hall and offer his arm. She always accepted it, but not willingly. Still feeling that he had failed Tinette, she had never been able to warm to him.

In good weather Nancy took a part of each day to go outside, leaning on first one and then another. Actually her favorite for these walks was Flora Stanton. Flora's strength helped her, and her silence allowed Nancy to bring memory into play.

"That is where I found that hook," she would think. Or "Cal planted that tree in 1875." Or "Black Thunder, are you behind that old shed?"

Conversely she also enjoyed walking with chatterbox Wanda. What sounded like sass and rudeness to others was funny to Nancy. She did not always laugh, but she always felt like it.

"Gran, pick up your old feet. Go kicking every stone and pebble. If you would shorten your dresses like everyone else, they wouldn't be catching on the bushes."

One day the two of then stood at the fence, looking at the pheasants.

"Wanda," asked her grandmother. "Do you miss Cal?"

"Yes."

"How much?"

Wanda could hardly believe it was happening to her, old happy-go-lucky, who-gives-a-darn Wanda. There was actually a lump in her throat, and as she looked at her grandfather's birds, tears stung her eyes. Presently, she was able to answer her grandmother's question.

"Bunches," she said.

Nancy threw back her head and crowed triumphantly.

"I knew it," she said.

CHAPTER THREE

Tinette

When Tinette O'Neil was a child she had been carried around on her father's arm. Later she had tagged him under her own steam, and accompanied him thither and yon whenever it was practical. At the time when unwelcome suitors had pursued her too avidly, he had taken her and her mother away for a change. When true love palled for her she had counted on his constant loyalty and he had not disappointed her. Even when she had brought Earl into the family, Calvin had been her strength. Not a word was ever spoken between them about her husband's infidelity, but Tinette had felt a sure sympathy from both of her parents as life continued.

Tinette sat in the warm cave one day culling the potatoes that were heaped in a wire-encased bin. She thought about her father, dead now for a few weeks, and gloried in his moral strength.

"I wonder," she thought, "if he was always strong of character or if it was something he had learned."

Calvin had never talked much about his early life, at least not to her. Once Nancy had told Tinette that it was her belief that Calvin's father, Raither O'Neil, had been worth a lot. In character was what she meant because she had told Tinette that he had insisted upon being with his son under adverse conditions.

Then again Nancy once made reference to an uncle of Calvin's. "That was a cheating rascal for sure," and went on to say she was glad that Calvin had not taken after him.

Tinette laughed to herself as the ludicrous thought came to her that perhaps Earl had taken after the uncle.

She had not spoken to Earl about her father's death, not a word. She might have asked him what he thought about Calvin's way of dividing his money among the children. Or she could have laughed with him over the change in her mother's attitude, "dolling up" as she did each day. The rest of the family had been grateful for the positive aspect of it, had smiled to see how sweet the old lady looked. But she had never asked Earl if he had even noticed.

Calvin and Earl had of late years matched themselves at many a game of dominoes and cards. Yet Tinette never offered to console her husband in the loss of his partner, certainly had never offered to "sit in" for her father.

Tinette tried to analyze her feelings, tried to ask herself why she had not tried to reach Earl in their time of intense grief. In tumbling the potatoes around, her hand touched one that was shriveled until its skin felt soft, even mushy. A rotten potato would contaminate every potato it touched. Why was not the opposite true? Why couldn't strong, crisp potatoes impart health to the weak, ailing ones?

Finished with her task, Tinette pulled the wire netting snugly over the bin. At her feet stood the bucket of culls that Ted would carry out to the pigs. For a moment she looked at them, then said to herself, "They are the throwaways, only fit — " She closed her eyes and shook her head. "I will not think such thoughts," she said. "These are potatoes, they are not people."

Yet, as she went up the steps, she could not keep the thought back. "Father could not perfect Earl in all these years, but will Earl touch Wanda?" Her mental picture was of a good potato resting next to —

"No." Tinette heard herself say the word, and as she leaned over to close the door she burst into sobs.

Ted and Priscilla were in the kitchen, and as Tinette

entered she thought to herself, "They will think I am weeping for Papa. Let them think it. In a way I am. Perhaps from now on, our loss of Papa will underlie every emotion."

Potatoes seemed to be the order of the day. St. Patrick's Day was coming up and Priscilla was helping Ted get the "eyes" ready for planting. They both looked sympathetically at Tinette as she sniffled across and out of the room. It was Saturday and there was to be a high school dance in honor of the Irish, although the actual day was still two days off.

The family had had a discussion that week on whether Wanda should be allowed to attend.

"Allowed?" she had yelled. "Who do you think you are talking to? Marguerite here? I am eighteen years old!"

Everyone talked at once, and Wanda put her hands over her ears. With the heel of her shoe she beat out a steady rhythm against the table leg. She even began to hum. All she could think of was the school song so that was the tune she hummed.

"It is entirely too close to our recent bereavement." — from Franklin.

"I don't think she will be expected to go. Everyone would be shocked." — from Ted.

"She might as well go out and dance on poor Grandfather's grave." — from Sara.

"It would be too cold." — from Marguerite.

"What is the proper length of mourning now?" — from Priscilla.

"The number of days is unimportant. We are talking about a dance." — from Sara.

"Calvin loved to dance." — from Nancy.

"How many want pie?" — from Tinette.

"I do." — from Earl.

All the time "a thing" was nagging at the back of Tinette's mind. There was something rankling her. She knew full well what it was, but it was as if it were behind

28

clouds or behind curtains, or behind a window that was steamed over. Curtains most aptly fit the situation — soft, gauzy curtains — because the force behind them kept billowing them out, almost but not quite letting "the thing" out.

Tinette went on much as usual. She sewed the yellow and pink blouses for her mother, she even made her a new "Sunday" dress of maroon silk faille which allowed the previous "Sunday" dress of heavy blue crepe to slip into "second best" place, thus freeing a light gray wool for everyday wear.

Although Priscilla looked after most of the housework, with Flora doing the actual job of cleaning, Tinette began a minute inspection of the house. From the slanted ceiling cubicle off the bathroom, she pulled several discarded items and had Franklin carry them into town for St. Mark's rummage sale. One day she ran back upstairs to get one more item and she found her mother in the bathroom.

"Oh, Mama," she said as she opened the door. "I didn't know you were up here."

"Back off, Tinette, and kindly close the door behind you."

"Just a minute, Mama, let me cross over to the attic room. I need to get — "

"Tinette! Use some modesty, please."

"I won't look, Mama, but Jim is waiting to take the load — "

"Tinette!"

Tinette backed off and closed the door. She went into Franklin's room on the left side of the hall to wait for her mother to leave the bathroom. Franklin's room was to the west and Tinette noticed that the blue curtains looked definitely faded from the evening sun. Stepping closer to measure by eyesight the exact size of the curtains, she mused, "I'll now have to get busy making new ones." She glanced out the window. Spring was not far off and the

29

day was pleasant. Under the big cottonwood in the side yard stood Ted and Priscilla. He was leaning back against the sturdy trunk and his circumspect wife was leaning on him, her body pressed so tightly to his that it looked as if he were wearing her apron. They kissed.

Tinette drew back from the window and said, "Well, that was a scene I never saw before, or ever expected to."

Nancy walked out of the bathroom at that moment, and Tinette ran in to grab the box she wanted. As she helped her mother down the stairs, she said, "Franklin's curtains look so old. I believe I shall ask Jim to wait while I run up and get them for the rummage sale."

"Don't do it."

"Why?"

"They will need to be washed. Starched and ironed, too. There will always be another rummage sale."

"Oh, I don't think they are dirty, Mama, just old."

"Everything gets dusty. You know that, Tinette."

They reached the ground floor and Nancy headed for the parlor.

"What will you put up to his windows, Tinette?" she asked.

"I have some of that ecru muslin that I used in Ted's room."

"Why not white? That is more respectable."

"The boys have never liked white curtains, Mama."

"Well, Priscilla does. Let her have white curtains."

"That is up to her and Ted. This is Franklin's room."

"I love Priscilla. And her grandmother meant so much to me."

"I know, Mama." When Tinette looked at Nancy, it seemed as if she looked sad. Deciding to cheer her up Tinette said, "When I looked out of Franklin's window, I saw Ted kiss Priscilla."

"Out in the yard?" Nancy's voice rose as she asked the question, and as she dropped onto the sofa she let her hands fall with a plop onto the lap of her pearl gray dress.

"Well, I'll be!" she said with a grin. "That girl is smart."

"How, Mama?"

"There are different, varyin' ways to get close to a husband, and she knows 'em all."

Tinette thought to herself, "How strange to hear Mama talk like this. And she even made her words sound different. More like Papa's." A smile came onto her face as she thought of her mother using the "facility" and demanding privacy. And it seemed to her that it was getting much harder for Nancy to descend the stairs. The thought came to her that the bathroom should have been added downstairs. Then the storeroom could have been left in its former size, a room that could really hold discards.

She ran back up to get the curtains, then took a moment to go into the girls' room at the front of the house. As usual Sara's half was as neat as a place that had never been used. Wanda's half was discouraging, bed not really made, covers only thrown back. Evidently she had been trying on her old spring dresses and a few were just thrown on a chair.

"Maybe those are the ones that don't fit her anymore," Tinette was thinking.

On the foot of Wanda's bed lay some carelessly tossed magazines, *Photoplay* and *Delineator*. This one appealed to Tinette and she lay back on the bed to look at it, on her side with one elbow propping her head and one hand free to turn pages.

On one page Tinette's glance was attracted to a house plan. "That reminds me a little of our house," she said. Then with a bit of a silent chuckle she added, "But this one is no farmhouse." For it was clearly a house plan drawn by an architect who worked for well-to-do city dwellers. At the bottom of the drawing readers were advised to turn to the next page for colored pictures of some of the rooms.

The aspect of the plan and the accompanying picture was what was called a "powder room." Tinette had never heard of that and was not interested in it per se, but this was a two-story house with a bathroom upstairs and a "facility" downstairs. As she closed the book the idea seemed to take hold of her and she was fascinated by the possibility.

Tinette lay back on the bed, resting her full body upon it by drawing up her knees beside her. "The Thing" that had been lying dormant for many weeks burst right out at her, demanding to be considered.

"The Thing" was Weston O'Neil. There he had stood, not as much as a yard before her. In 1891, thirty-three years ago, she had told him "Goodbye." There was not a yard between them that day, nor a foot, or even an inch. Like Ted and Priscilla. "So that was what had brought him to my mind so forcefully," Tinette thought.

As she lay on Wanda's bed, constantly wrinkling and then smoothing out a small section of the dark green coverlet (chosen and insisted upon by Sara), Tinette's thoughts ran on. "I'll never see him again. He understood me and he will do as I ask. I know he will. He will never come back now."

Tinette thought of all the things she had taught herself to think about Weston. "How wicked he was to possess a wife and yet pursue me. He was that all right. He looked like his distant cousin, Calvin, enough to be close kin.

"Lately we hear of divorce among respectable people. Look at Flora's cousin Lottie. A beautiful girl and one who was never spoken of derogatorily. People respected her and she divorced old Lute Cribbs. Flora said that Lottie had even remarried someone in Topeka and not one soul ever looked at Lottie as sullied. Of course, Lute had been a drunkard, and Lottie was right in wanting to get little Andy away from his influence and treatment.

"But Lottie had survived divorce with absolutely no scandal. Why hadn't Weston way back then suggested divorce as a solution to their heartache? Oh yes, he had promised his mother. Also she had money. So what?

How did that help Weston? Was money more than love? But, of course, there was the promise to his mother. Anyway, could I ever have married a divorced man?"

Tinette turned over on her back and closed her eyes. Her shapely legs hung off the bed but the change of position felt good to them. They even pulled at her back a little bit and the slight stretching relaxed her. She realized she was falling asleep and she did not care. Her last thought was, "I did not react to seeing Weston at all. I felt nothing. He evoked no response whatever."

Her nap lengthened and she even dreamed. She was standing very close to a man who had thick curls, part of them were black and part of them were white. Emanating from him was an odor of wet wool, and in her dream she realized that her face was pressed against the man's tweed coat. She pushed herself away and then she could see that the man was Weston. A feeling of intense love passed between them.

"Tinette," a not-too-gentle voice spoke.

She thought, "Surely Weston's voice didn't used to sound like that."

She opened her eyes to find that her husband was standing beside her. He wanted her to know that he was going to walk into town. As Earl left the room, Tinette pulled herself to a sitting position. She realized that her legs, dangling from the bed, were asleep. Besides that, the room was cold and so was she. It hurt to put weight on her feet, and her whole body moved stiffly now. She stomped her feet and turned her torso from left to right, and gradually felt able to go downstairs.

As she descended, she glanced over the bannister and envisioned a door, like in the house plan, opening into a "powder room." But the door she pictured opened into her parents' room.

Would her mother ever allow that? Besides that, a fancy "powder room" did not fit into Tinette's idea at all.

She entered the bedroom just as Nancy was awakening

from a nap. Tinette helped her up and helped her get readjusted to a vertical world. All of the time her eyes had been upon the south side of the room, the side where her parents' bed used to be in other days. Now a tall chifferobe stood there, a large piece of handsome black walnut that held Nancy's clothes. There was even one suit of Calvin's in there. He had been buried in his good suit, and his other clothes had been passed on to Jim Stanton.

Beside the chifferobe stood a glassed-in chest, about half the size of the clothes's chest, and in it were three beautiful hats. One was rather small, covered with green, gold and blue feathers. One was a gray velvet and above the narrow brim was a purple velvet rose. The other hat was waiting for summer as it was a floppy-brimmed leghorn. It was the only one that Nancy did not like.

"What are you staring at, Tinette?"

"Mama, I want to move that south wall, or the biggest part of it, and bring it a few feet this way."

"What in the world, Tinette! I will not have my room disturbed."

"You don't need that much room, and I'll tell you what I want to put into that space."

"What space?"

"When we move the wall in — "

"I am not going to have a wall moved. I planned the size of this room myself and Calvin said that I would never have to change it."

"Mama! Papa could not have said such a thing because no one ever considered changing it."

"Tinette. Are you telling me that you know what my husband said to me when we were in here alone?"

"Now, Mama, listen to the reason I have for wanting to move that wall."

"Never. I will not stand for the moving of a wall. Here or anywhere."

"I want to put in a bathroom for you in that space."

"What?"

"It would not be wide like the one upstairs, but its length will allow for a tub and a commode, with a lavatory opposite. A door can open into your room and another one into the hall."

Nancy O'Neil turned and walked to the door. As she opened it, she faced Tinette and asked, "When can you start work on it?"

CHAPTER FOUR

Earl

*B*efore Earl Norris had found his wife asleep on Wanda's bed, he had been at the desk in their room trying to organize some recent notes he had taken on the period of history that had preceded the War of 1812. At one time he had wanted to touch on many such periods in history, giving his own interpretations. But gradually he had begun to see that to study and write on this one age was quite enough.

He had begun his work as it centered around the close of the 18th century, and this was largely because he had been able to amass more books on that particular era. When Miss Mary Pattison had died, she had left him a legacy that had enabled him to buy books and off and on through the years he had worked on studying them, then on condensing the information.

For days, maybe weeks at a time, Earl would read first one book and then another. Sometimes he would receive rental books from a firm in New York City, books that had maybe only a page or two devoted to the years that followed the Revolutionary War. Some barely touched on the War of 1812. But he would pore over these, take notes, then compare them with the books that went into his subject in depth.

Sometimes he would toss it all aside, "letting the Devil take it," as he said. Maybe nearly a year would go by before he would feel a spark of interest again. Earl gave up dentistry completely not long after Mary Pattison's death, though he held onto the office for a while. Later he sold his equipment. Then the only contact he had with his former office was to walk by it and wonder how he had stood the work at all.

When Tinette had first met Earl Norris, he had been made known to her as a dentist and history buff. Old Doc Pattison had told her that "Earl can read a book the neatest of any man I ever knew." It was true. He had a talent for understanding what an author was saying and even for reading between the lines and divining interpretations left unsaid in the book. The interpretations he was able to give to the events on which he was writing were the best parts of his work.

As the years passed, his periods of avidity for writing became shorter and farther apart. By the time Calvin O'Neil died, Earl Norris' work was at a standstill. All he wanted to do then was put his study books in order and write a very few concluding pages to his own brief work.

"I guess this is long enough anyway for just one little part of history," he said to no one but himself.

He had felt an urge to breathe fresh air and to feel it wash over his face — sweet spring air. That was why he had looked for his wife, to let her know that he was going to walk into town.

For many years Earl had lived in apparent non-shame that he contributed not one thing to the livelihood of the family. There was a time when Mary Pattison's bequeathment brought, through sour memories, a measure of embarrassment to him. But that was short-lived. His wife had removed herself so completely from him that he really felt that it had been he who had been wronged. She owed him something. He had married her and she was his wife. The whole family was against him. Let them bear the brunt of the result of their mistreatment. Let them shoulder the cost, the entire responsibility.

More and more Earl had settled in as a loafer, until his parasitic life began to make him cynical. First he had begun to feel twinges now and then of guilt which at the beginning he was able to shrug off. Then this reaction became difficult and he turned to blame. "It's Tinette's fault. It's all of 'em's fault." Only in recent months had he turned to cynicism.

The years had gone quickly, and in spite of it all, not at all unbearably. He had enjoyed the children, Wanda most of all, until they had begun to branch out with outside interests that excluded him. Tinette had interacted pleasantly, if not in the bedroom at least in the kitchen, and often they had indulged in discussions of their various reading materials. The editorial page of the *Kansas City Star* gave them many topics for conversation. Then in late years he had really enjoyed and looked forward to his daily card-table event. Calvin was better at cards, but often Earl would win at dominoes.

Surmising that it was the old man's death which had brought about his own present restlessness, Earl said to himself, "It's too bad." He felt he had not been included in the family's mourning, as though he had experienced no grief. Realizing that Calvin had meant more to Tinette than he, her own husband, had, he sensed that rancor was taking over his outlook. He felt spiteful and could not bring himself to express sympathy even to Tinette.

On this particular day Earl Norris felt stifled by the house, by his room, and by the work lying on his desk. Seating himself with a reluctant urgency, he brought his work to a hasty conclusion. He had intended this summary to be merely the end of one section of his book. Now he recognized it as the final word.

Leaving his desk top in order for the first time in years, books piled on the shelves above it and papers either thrown away or crammed into drawers, Earl Norris left to find Tinette. Under his arm he carried a large envelope of papers which he had carelessly stapled together.

When he told Tinette that he was going to walk to town, she did not give an immediate response and he did not wait for one. He walked briskly away and within fifteen minutes was standing outside the newspaper office.

Editor Wilson had recently taken into his employ a young lady who was an excellent typist. On one previous occasion she had typed up an essay for Earl and he had been impressed with her work. She had a room with a family in town and on her own time she would undertake to do extra typing for people. At the time he had been introduced to her, Mr. Wilson had mentioned that Maxine would type for people personally. Earl had not needed to have an essay typed, it was actually to be a part of the entire work, but on impulse he decided to try her. She not only typed it excellently, but did a fair amount of editing and changing, having the confidence of youth in addition to her ability. Earl realized that the result was an improvement.

On this day he took a moment to straighten his tie and button his jacket. He removed his cap and smoothed back his white hair. Still a fine looking fellow, he glanced at his reflection in the shop window somewhat vainly. He liked his slender nose and his fatless chin.

Inside he asked to speak to Maxine. A fellow sitting on a high stool, by a table of type, nodded his head to one side, and Earl's eyes followed the move. Sitting at a desk was Maxine, not typing a copy but contemplating it. Earl stepped over to her and was pleased when she stood and greeted him so pleasantly. He told her that in the envelope was a piece of historical writing. He said that actually it was to be a short book, and it needed to be typed. And he added, er-ah-perhaps it needed to be looked over. The girl understood and accepted the work.

Maxine's youthful smile and her friendly manner gave Earl a real lift. When he stepped outside of the office there was a grin on his face.

He had gone nearly half a block before he realized that he had not yet put his cap back on.

As he walked down Commercial Street, he passed his old office space. It was now used by a milliner, but above it, on the second floor, was where the present dentist had fixed up his office. The sight of the dentist's sign slowed him down. He said to himself, "I was a failure." It was the first time that such a thought had ever occurred to him, and he felt depressed because of it.

Slowly, heavily, he walked on another couple of blocks and came to stand in front of a large yellow frame house. Many people, including himself, still referred to it as "The Pattison House" although both of the Pattisons had been dead for years. Earl crossed the street and lowered himself to the curb. Lying in the street was a branch. He picked it up and with deliberate snaps began to remove each twig. Occasionally he would stop the process and look over at the house.

"That house was the cause of mine and Tinette's trouble," he was thinking. "Mary kept at me to go see her. I didn't even like her. It was the house I liked and wanted."

Earl's memory showed him once more the small dining room where Mary would sit whenever he visited there, sit and pour tea. In his mind's eye he also saw the stairway and the room upstairs where Mary would lead him. This memory irked him and made him yank off the twigs with a snap.

"If only Doc had lived, it would never have happened." Earl's mind would not let go of the picture of his infidelity. He shook his head as if to shake the memory, but it clung.

"How could I do it? She was old, a skinny old maid. And then she did not leave me the house," he thought with distaste.

He got to his feet and started back to the place he had called "home" for many years. At the tracks he had to wait for a freight train to pass, and as he stood there hearing the clickety-clack, he was made to think of the train ride he took to Atchison years ago, to be with Mary overnight.

"How could I have done it?" he asked several times as he walked to the edge of town. He felt that going back was the most difficult task he had ever had to perform. Going up the Walton Hill, his feet slowed to a plodding pace as it came to him that no word of accusation had ever passed from the O'Neils to him. He hoped that the children had never realized what had occurred. Reaching the flat space that Calvin had dubbed the "long stretch," he began to pick up his feet and hurry along. When he entered the house he went right to his room and there he stayed all evening.

Earl was suprised to be called to the phone early the next day. It was Maxine. She had read the entire manuscript and wanted to tell him how thrilled she was with it. Complying with her request he said he would be able to pay her a visit Sunday afternoon. She said she had a key to the office and that was where she would be.

The three days until Sunday passed, and Earl had sat them out. Like his mother-in-law in the parlor, he sat for hours in the porch swing. To the east of the kitchen Calvin had long ago built a small porch. The kitchen door to the porch was seldom used, especially in winter. When hot weather returned the door was left standing open, and the screen door was opened and closed more often.

But winter was barely leaving at this point, and hardly anyone ever so much as glanced out to the porch. Calvin had bought a sturdy swing one day, one just the width of two people, and he had hung it from the ceiling of the east porch. In the yard sat a sturdy push swing, one wide seat of it facing its counterpart. The little children had loved to swing back and forth in it, taking turns at standing up as they played "conductor taking tickets from the riders." It was Calvin's idea that the parents or grandparents would sit in the new swing and watch.

But as Earl now recalled, he could not think of one time when he and Tinette had enjoyed it together or even alone. He could remember times in their lives when congeniality had been theirs, but in part of those times Tinette had been pregnant and too ill to want the movement of a swing. Other times she always seemed too busy and they would have their conversational interchanges in the kitchen while she baked pies or cleaned the big range.

Now Earl sought the side porch because of its hideaway qualities. He would push the swing back with his feet, neatly covered with polished brown oxfords, then let it ride for awhile under its own momentum. Maxine did not enter into his cogitations but his history book did. What would he call it? What would he do about marketing it?

The last of Earl's cash had gone for the rental books and their postage. What he had left was negligible. But he had to talk to a publisher. Some time back, one of the books he had rented from New York gave listings of publishing houses there. Earl had copied the names and addresses of those he thought might at some later time be a contact for him. The list was in his pocket right now.

In Earl's mind was the idea of taking the manuscript personally to these publishers. Now that someone had read it and had realized that it had merit — Maxine was no dumb girl. She was sharp and alert, and she had come to Waterville from a business school in Wichita. She knew what she was doing. Actually the manuscript must be worth more than he thought.

On Sunday Earl Norris awakened before dawn. Afraid to disturb Tinette, not that he felt guilty about the manuscript and the planned afternoon concerning it, but she would undoubtedly ask why he was up so early. He did not want to take away one iota of the magic of expected events by voicing them.

Wanda had slept in the room with her parents first in a crib, then on a low bed for a long time. Finally about the time Ted married, Tinette had allowed Wanda to move across the hall with Sara, each sleeping in a large bed across the room from one another. Then Tinette had purchased twin beds for herself and Earl, but leaving her usual bed beside another wall. It was her cot-size bed on which she had slept most of her life and it could now become a naptime refuge.

The nervous man lay still until his wife arose, dressed and left the room. Then with unusual energy he also arose. He dressed in his best suit, shirt, and tie. Before leaving the room he made up both beds, just to have someting to do. Then he walked down the stairs slowly with affected dignity, almost making himself laugh. Removing any hint of a smile he walked back to the kitchen and poured himself a cup of coffee.

When Priscilla entered the room, he told her that he would like to accompany her and Marguerite to church.

"What?" Tinette asked. "You're a little early for Easter, Earl."

"Not much," he replied.

The three of them set out for church together, actually for Sunday School first, and Earl said he would wait in the car until church time. His granddaughter was a pretty child with the same sweet nature as her mother. Both were still dressed in winter dresses but the child's dress was of white wool, and with the early sweet peas she carried she bespoke spring. They were a lovely pair and Earl was proud to join them.

He heard not one word of the sermon, nor did he remember to pray, not even in behalf of his written creation. His entire thinking was centered on a means by which he could get himself to New York City. However, his attention was captured by the sound of a sweet, clear voice singing every note in sharp precision even though some words were a bit off. He had never realized before that Marguerite had such a talent for song.

After church Earl declined the ride home. "I have a hankering to eat at Weaver's Hotel today," he told Priscilla. "Just tell Tinette to go on ahead with dinner and I'll be out later."

At the hotel Earl took his time eating, then went for a walk around town before finally arriving at the *Telegraph* office. True to her word, Maxine was waiting. Actually, she was just finishing the typing of his manuscript. She was excited about his work. She had edited it, changed it a bit here and there, polished up a phrase or two, corrected now and then an error of grammar or punctuation, but in the main it had evoked a glowing response.

"Mr. Norris," she said, "make no delay in getting this before the eyes of a publisher, a publishing house that deals in history, or perhaps in college textbooks."

Maxine Holz went on to say that she had urgent typing to do for a student at Manhattan, but that her good wishes would go with him. They shook hands and Earl departed with his typed and carboned manuscript, never once offering to pay her. He never even asked what the price was for all her work, although he had a faint idea that she had typed far into each night to have it ready for him.

Now the problem was acute. A young lady fresh out

of school, coming from the large town of Wichita, had recognized his work as a useful one. She had even suggested the possibility of its being used as a textbook. A college textbook! She had urged him to take it to a publisher of such books. That would be in New York City. How to get there?

Earl walked home and every step of the way he was thinking of money. Where could he get some? Was there any avenue open to him? He thought of selling his books, but instantly knew that was impractical. There was not one soul around who would want his books, and even if there were by chance such a person, the books would not bring a price that would be of any help.

As he got close to the creek that ran across the little pasture, he saw the sheep. They were lambing. How much did a lamb bring, he wondered. Farther on he saw the orchard and impractically wished that he had time to cut down trees and sell them for lumber. At the driveway he saw the pheasants but knew he could never get them sacked up without being discovered by the family.

He walked past the birds and stood by the windmill a moment. Coming in with the cows was Wanda riding Pony, a beautiful horse with a fancy saddle. It was only a cow pony, and Earl wished that she had been riding the mustang instead. But this was his opportunity and not to be quibbled over.

Wanda easily herded the cows into the corral, then answered her father's beckoning gesture.

"What is it, Dad?"

"I'm of a notion to take a ride on Pony myself."

"Why, Dad! What a notion! When in the world have you last ridden?"

"Don't be smart, my girl. I knew how to sit a horse before you were born."

"But lately?"

"Will you get down?"

"Sure thing, Dad. Can I help you up?"

"Now that remark makes me feel stubborn. Go on to the house. Go on! I'm going to stand here until you do."

"Then?"

"Then I'm going to have me a ride."

The girl gave her carefree laugh, shrugged her shoulders, and ran for the house. She called back, "Will you unsaddle Pony?"

"Never fear," he called back.

Earl Norris put his precious envelope inside his jacket, holding it closed to his body, and mounted the pony. First, he took a short ride up to the pasture through the lane of trees where the cows had just walked. He rode slowly up and then more slowly back.

He talked to himself, asking, "Now where will I be apt to get the most money? This is a good horse and I know that Calvin always bought the best when he could. And look at this saddle. A real beauty. I believe I shall head for Nebraska. Someone in Lincoln should give me a fair price. A well-saddled pony, a strong pony, that is no small thing, and I'd be going northeast to get a train for New York anyway."

As the determined man let all scruples go, he set his goal for the publishing houses of New York City. He turned Pony eastward, spurred him, raced by the house and out the driveway. His granddaughter playing in the side yard saw him turn towards town and ride away.

CHAPTER FIVE

Franklin

*F*ranklin Norris was considered "dry" by many people who were too kind to admit that he was "boring." As the third member of the trilogy he was considered to be the "baby." Of course, by the time Wanda was added to the family, Franklin was a tall eleven-year-old and not at all given to babyish ways.

In some ways, the younger boy rivaled his older brother in maturity. At least many of the teachers at Waterville School looked to him as being of a more responsible nature. Perhaps they really meant "studious" because although none of the Norris children ever reneged on homework, Franklin's was always of a better caliber than Ted's.

Franklin went in for detail and for almost exhaustive thoroughness. If a history assignment asked, "If you had been a senator in 1863, would you have been able to give a reasonable accounting for your support of Lincoln's Edict of Emancipation?" The students at the Norris abode would have been working out answers from various angles.

Ted's answer would have taken hardly any time at all, as in addition to the heading on his homework paper the only word to appear would have been, "Yes."

Sara would have prepared a paragraph of such a subjective nature that the teacher would think her pupil was upbraiding her for questioning Lincoln's action.

But scholar Franklin would accept the challenge, plus

added ones not even implied in the question. His teacher always saved his homework and test papers until last if they were essay style because she might have to wade through several pages of stances, refutations, and rebuttals.

Franklin never had enjoyed farm work, and while he understood that as long as he lived on the farm he must do his share, he was glad when the day came that he was employed as Mr. Logback's grocery clerk. It was not that he was ever expected to pay for his livelihood on the farm, it was just that he must be busy at some kind of work.

The quality that Franklin lacked was a sense of humor. Grandfather O'Neil had excelled in this area. And while always understanding his wit, his wife Nancy did not always laugh at it, and her occasional scurries into humor were of the dry variety, but funny nonetheless. Ted and Wanda both laughed frequently, but Franklin seldom did. It was the flaw in his nature that made people say he was too serious.

When America went into the war in 1917, Ted received a deferment because operation of a farm was considered essential employment. But Franklin enlisted. When he went to enlist, he did so over the pleas of his mother to wait. She wanted Franklin to register as a farmer, too, but Franklin registered as "business clerk." His mother urged patience, told him to wait until he was called. As a reply she received an oration of such strength and length as to why he had to enlist that she limply gave in.

He was sent to Fort Riley, Kansas. There he made such a name for himself that his entire tour of duty was spent in his native state as company clerk. Upon being mustered out, he collapsed with the flu before he ever reached home. Having been carried back to the fort, he stayed not only until his strength had returned but until all of the sick soldiers were again on the feet that carried them homeward. As did his school records, now Army reports delineated Franklin Norris as "thorough."

When the ex-soldier saw an opportunity to go in on a grocery store enterprise with Waterville denizen Arlo Frye, he prepared a set of reasons why he should be allowed to do so. He prepared it as carefully as if it were an airtight brief to be presented in court by an earnest lawyer. Tinette and her father listened to the long oration, but none of it was necessary. Not the prepared brief or the speech. Calvin O'Neil was ready and wanting to supply the cash.

Thus Waterville's general store came to be known as "Norris and Frye." Periodically, that is at regular intervals (nothing haphazard about any of Franklin's dealings), Mr. F. Norris would make cash payments on his loan to his grandfather. Calvin kept the actual payments, but every bit of interest that Franklin paid was set aside, and when the debt was repaid Calvin gave back all of the interest money to the young man.

Mourning his grandfather's death was a natural thing for Franklin. The loss hit him as a square blow, and for several days he gave in to his grief. Then he was able to gather himself together, look at it as a part of his life that had passed, and turn his attention to work, to social obligations, and to the family.

Franklin remembered, actually never in his life forgot, how much Nancy had meant to his childhood happiness. But he was not a man to attach any obligation to such memories. At the table he took it for granted that she was part of the set, but it was a rare day that he ever sat down beside her in the parlor for a visit.

The rest of the family he took as a matter of course. Abiding in the same house as they were, he met them at meals, but that was about the extent of his contact. He felt close to his mother and looked upon himself as a dutiful son upon whom she could always rely, and of whom she was justly proud. To her he even offered affection. This usually took the form of a good-morning kiss.

But not even to his mother did he disclose the fact of his very fine profits from the store. Actually, it was not difficult for any of them to surmise the second son was doing well. Improvements in the store, as well as the new blue Buick, bespoke prosperity.

As for Earl Norris, Franklin accepted him as a genial enough man who puzzled him with his lack of initiative. As a boy Franklin had never received criticism or rebuke from his father, and on occasion his mind would flash back to early days when Earl would provide hours of fun at games that especially pleased boys.

After the death and burial of his grandfather, Franklin began to get a different glimpse of Earl. His father was now the oldest male in the household, and at age sixty-six was showing age. His hair was white but he still had a classic facial appearance and his skin had not begun to wrinkle or sag. Still there was something about the man that evoked pity. His being seemed to droop and it depressed Franklin. Somewhere in the back of his mind he had a vague idea of reaching out to his dad, maybe even spending a little time with him.

It was time for Sunday evening supper on a spring day in 1924, and the various members of the family were gathering in the dining room. Dusk had passed and although there was still a bit of light outside, the house looked gloomy inside.

A few years earlier, Calvin O'Neil had, with the help of Franklin's business contacts, ordered a fellow to be at the farm one day to install a complete system of Delco lights for the house. By now the electric lights were an accustomed and taken-for-granted commodity, at least by everyone from Ted down. The two older ladies still marveled at the magic of them. Nancy especially kept recalling the days that preceded even the use of coal-oil lamps, the days when she and Calvin had even been too poor to indulge in candlelight. And now and then she would tell and retell about the nights when only Black Thunder's pipe shed a light.

On this evening Sara was placing a platter of pressed chicken on the table and asking Franklin as he entered to turn on the light. In each room the lights were set aglow by the turn of a round button on the wall, sort of a box, the type that held snuff. Sara's brother complied by reaching his long arm across the buffet to the switch. Not a sound was made as the button brought the lights into play. No click, no snap, just a silent turn of the switch.

Ted had come in from milking and was scrubbing his hands and arms, leaning over the sink to splash water onto his face. He was glad that Jim Stanton had arrived in time to finish the job for him as it was a task Ted disliked. His wife and his mother had helped Sara get the table ready, and Tinette was just placing a large spoon in a bowl of potato salad.

"I'll get Grandmother," Sara said and left the room whose light also dimly lit the sitting room.

"It's suppertime, Grandmother," she said as she reached the parlor door.

"How could I know that?"

"What do you mean, Grandmother? How could you know what?"

"How could I see that it was suppertime in this dark room?"

"Shall I turn the light on then?"

"Oh, of course, stupid," said Wanda who had raced Marguerite down the stairs and was standing in the hall.

"Wanda," spoke Sara in her precise and now offended tone, "I am not stupid. To me it is useless to turn on a light when all we are going to do is and leave the room."

51

In the moment it took to talk about it, little Marguerite danced her fairy-like self over to the switch and had turned it on.

"There, Great-grandmother. There you are. Shall I help you get up?"

Nancy offered her hand to the child and laughed as she stood on her feet. It pleased her so much that Marguerite had ignored both of her aunts in order to help her, that she caressed the girl. They were not far from being the same size.

At the dining table each took his or her place. The table was oval in shape and more than large enough to accommodate ten chairs. At one end sat Tinette and Marguerite, with Ted and Priscilla to the child's right, then Wanda. Next came Nancy, alone now but with Calvin's chair standing beside her. To her right sat Franklin and Sara. The chair to Tinette's left stood empty.

"Where is Dad?" asked Ted.

And at the same moment, "Why is Dad late?" from Sara. "And on Sunday evening, too."

"Now why would that make any difference?" from Wanda in her insolent tone.

"Not make a difference when our father is not at the table?" Sara replied in a huff.

"No, Sara. Why would the day make a difference? Is it a worse offense to be late on Sunday?" Wanda's sneering grunt of a laugh irked her sister tremendously.

"I'll see about him, Mother," Sara spoke angrily and pushed her chair back noisily.

"Shall I say grace, Grandmother?" Marguerite asked cautiously.

"Well — "

"Go ahead, Honey," her father urged.

"Bless this house and all of us in it. Thank you, Jesus, for our food."

Sara was practically running to get back to the table to tell them that Earl was nowhere in sight. Ted, too, got up, saying he would go outside to see if he was around anywhere. But before he could leave, his daughter spoke.

"Oh, I saw Granddad leave."

"Leave?" several voices asked.

"What do you mean, Honey?" Priscilla thought to ask.

"I was out there," pointing to the east yard, "and all at once I heard Pony's feet going fast. Granddad was on him."

"Which way did he head?"

Marguerite gave a backward shake of her head and said, "That way. To town."

"Perhaps he left his hat or something at the hotel and just thought of it," Tinette suggested.

"Was there to be a church service tonight?"

"I thought you had Pony out for a ride, Wanda," said Ted as he sat down again.

"I rode him up after the cows."

"Did you put the saddle away as I asked you to?"

"No."

"Why not?"

"I never had a chance."

"What do you mean?"

"Can't anyone ever just leave me alone? Damn!"

"Wanda!" exclaimed nearly every person in the room, and Sara added that no one in the family used that forbidden word.

"Forbidden by whom?" yelled Wanda who had learned to apply the rules of grammar fairly well. "And you are mistaken besides, dear sister. Our father's speech is full of 'damns' and words just like it."

"That, Wanda, is not so," Franklin corrected.

"I never have heard him say one bad word, Wanda, and I am older than you." Sara spoke as if even she had been insulted by her sister's accusation.

"That is because neither of you ever go near him enough to hear anything he says."

"No lady — "

"Shut up, Sara!" Wanda yelled the words.

Ted brought his fist down upon the table with enough force to spill coffee into the saucer. "Wanda, I asked you why you did not put Pony's saddle away."

Wanda ignored her brother for the moment and pled, "Mom, doesn't Dad say words like 'damn'?"

"Wanda, dear, please do not pattern your speech after anyone who uses inferior words or even improper grammar. But, yes, you have heard your father say words that he did not really want you to hear."

Marguerite nodded and whispered, leaning over towards Tinnette, "We tell the truth, don't we, Grandmother?" She received a sly wink in return because the two of them had one day caught Earl in a temper when he used "the" words.

Mollified, Wanda told Ted what had happened when she came in from the corral, and how she had not dreamed that her father was leaving the place.

"Well, we won't wait supper. May I please have the applesauce?"

"Certainly, Gran."

Ted sat up that evening with his mother, and when Earl had not returned by midnight, Ted went upstairs to consult Franklin. The brothers went downstairs together, and Franklin told Tinette that all he knew to do was to call Mr. Wilson, who had one day mentioned to him that Earl had carried a packet of history writings into the newspaper office to be typed and carboned.

Tinette felt they should not bother the editor at night on such a flimsy clue, so they all decided to go to bed. Early the next morning the trio met in the kitchen. Franklin stood at the phone, rang it, and asked central to get Mr. Wilson for him. From this gentleman they learned that Maxine Holz had previously arranged to meet and discuss the typing with Mr. Norris on the day before.

When breakfast was over, Franklin and Sara, who had been apprised with the others of the latest development, left for town. It was earlier than usual, and Ted said that the girls could walk in later as it was not cold out.

Nancy had arisen and was having her morning coffee in the parlor as Wanda and Marguerite left for school. Tinette was closing the door behind them when she heard three sharp rings of the phone. That was their ring, but many a lady along the way would be "listening in." Thus all Franklin said was that he had to come back home for a minute, but Sara would stay at the store.

What Franklin had to tell was news indeed. Tinette had asked her mother to go into the kitchen with her and Priscilla to have her breakfast. She said "the boys" might be in soon with word of Earl's whereabouts. Nancy stifled a "Humph" and complied.

The news was that Franklin had seen Maxine Holz, an engaging girl, he told them. She had been very enthusiastic about Earl's "history book" as she called it, and admitted that she had sort of pointed him to publishing houses in New York City.

Franklin then asked at the depot if his dad had taken a train. He had not, but the kid who swept out the depot said that when he was coming in from grubbing around at the cemetery, he had seen Mr. Norris riding north on the Marysville road. The Norris family agreed that road led to many places and they had best wait.

The real news came later. When the family gathered for supper, Ted told about the phone call they had received late that afternoon. A man from Beatrice had called, saying he had recently purchased a pony and saddle from a Mr. Earl Norris.

Later he had been told by a neighbor that the horse belonged to a Mr. Calvin O'Neil over at Waterville. The fellow told Ted that he had felt odd about the transaction all along because Mr. Norris had been willing to take any price at all, saying he was going to Lincoln to get a train for New York. The fellow on the phone said he did not want to keep either of the purchases if the pony rightly belonged to someone else. Just so he got his money back and the price of the phone call.

Franklin asked Mr. Frye to open up the store the next day as he needed to take Ted up to Nebraska just as soon as the banks opened. Tinette insisted that the money be taken from her account. No one really contested her decision. They were all just glad that the money was forthcoming. When Ted arrived home that evening, everyone went out to meet him in order to give Pony a suitable, affectionate welcome.

As for news from Earl himself, it was only a little while in coming. The author was in New York City and out of luck, a penny post card declaring the news for all of Waterville to hear if the postmistress cared to read and tell. Earl had not really had enough money to keep him for long, and he wrote that he needed cash to live on until he could sell his manuscript.

At supper that night it was decided that Franklin should take the train to New York City and bring his father home. On the very next day Ted took Franklin to work, because when the eastbound train pulled into town Franklin Norris was to board it. The brothers shook hands at the store, and Ted told Sara, who had ridden with her brothers, that Priscilla would be in after her at closing time and any other day that Sara did not care to walk.

Sara went into the store and started to get her "goods" department ready for the day. But Franklin walked over to the newspaper office to see if Miss Holz was in yet. She was not, "thankfully," thought Franklin. He had plenty of time to meet her as she departed from her boarding home, and the two of them walked slowly back to her office.

Franklin Norris, age thirty, was in love. No doubt about it. Miss Maxine Holz, age twenty-one, had captured his heart. She, who had been impressed by the book of the older Mr. Norris, was much more impressed by the self of the younger Mr. Norris. Actually she was enamored of him. She sent him to New York feeling he must hurry back.

The family received two phone calls and two letters from their men in New York City. Then a week after Easter, they received the men themselves. Earl came back broken. His appearance evoked pity from the family and he went to his room to avoid them. His wife went with him and asked about his manuscript, hearing then that it had been left with a publisher who had acted somewhat interested. Tinette eased his homecoming and erased his debacle, at least from ever being referred to. Earl was very grateful.

But Franklin came home excited with a brand new love, and he called upon Maxine to discuss it. New York City, he told her, had won his heart. What he wanted to do was live there as a clothier. She let him know that she was not loathe to living there herself.

CHAPTER SIX

Wanda

Wanda Norris felt a certain amount of relief at her father's return, but problems were mounting so fast that she had trouble heeding any situation but her own.

For one thing, after she had definitely attended the St. Patrick's Day dance, Ted had caught her outside alone where he was able to talk to her without the constant family interference.

"Wanda, I for one know that you did not come home until three o'clock. Three hours after midnight!"

"Oh? What else do you know?"

Grabbing hold of her arm he said, "Sass is what we can do without, girl. And since you asked, I'll tell you that I happen to know that Mother is very grieved over it."

"Anything else, big boy?"

"Yes, there is." Ted's hand tightened on her slender arm and he gave her a slight shake. "Yes indeed, there is something else. You were brought home by Toot Salem."

"Why are you telling me things that I already know?"

"Wanda." Ted's voice softened and he dropped his hand from her arm. "I am pleading with you. That fellow is scum. You know how he got his name? Because he is always on a toot with bootleg whiskey."

"He never offered me any."

"He will ruin your reputation. A decent girl would not be seen with him."

"I am decent and don't be mistaken about it."

She turned and walked slowly, with her head defiantly high, towards the house. Toot was fun to be with. But it was true he was shunned by most of the kids at Waterville High. At the dance the other boys had not cut in and she had noticed that. Afterwards she had felt uncomfortable around the small group that lingered to sneak drinks with Toot. Maybe she had better take Ted's advice. But she would not let him know. Not for anything.

There was a crowd north of Waterville, from up and around Hanover, that was fun. She had met them at dances. It was true that they were looked upon as a fast crowd, but she had never heard liquor mentioned in connection with them. Several of the boys had taken a shine to Wanda, one of the girls had told her, and she decided to give them a try.

The family did not like the idea of the youngest being out every few nights. But if there was a dance up north, nothing could keep her from going. The school year was well into May and she had not even spoken to Toot Salem for a few weeks. He felt a mean streak coming over him. How could he pay her back?

One day, actually two days before the junior-senior banquet, the high school superintendent called Wanda into his office. It seemed that the sewing teacher had checked into the girls' lockers and had found among Wanda's belongings a bottle of moonshine with a note that said, "Thanks for the snort, Toot." Apparently Wanda's unorthodox behavior made her suspect. The superintendent did not want to condemn or even believe that it was not a prank. A denial from another type girl would have sounded plausible. But Wanda's defiant nature was against her.

Of course, she denied any knowledge of it, but had to admit to having had contact with Toot socially and in the school halls. But when the superintendent said he would have to speak to her mother, Wanda lost all composure.

"You don't believe me, that I knew nothing about what had been placed in my locker. You don't believe me."

"It is just that I feel that your fine mother, Mrs. Norris, should know about this."

"You actually believe that worthless, cheating, lying Toot Salem! Against my word. Why, you are no better than Toot yourself. You are as unethical as he is."

"Wanda," the man said as he rose from behind his desk. "I demand an apology."

"Well, you will never get it."

"I will have an apology before I can allow you to graduate."

"Never."

"I shall have to send you home now. You must deliver your apology in person before graduation. Even before you can attend the banquet."

"Do you think that I would actually come to graduation and accept a diploma from your hand?"

"Wanda. You must do two things. You must give me an apology in person, and you must attend the exercises in order to graduate from Waterville High School."

"Never."

"You will never receive a high school diploma."

"Keep your diploma. Keep your ring, too."

Wanda Norris took off the high school ring which she had worn as proudly as the other would-be graduates, and tossed it onto the man's desk. Without retrieving a single item of her possessions, the girl walked out of the building and headed home.

At home the family went into virtual spasms at the news. Tinette took it the hardest. She begged and pled for Wanda to change her decision, and then sat in the sitting room crying, visibly shaking in her state of shock. Hearing her weep, her mother called to her.

"Come sit in the parlor with me, Tinette. We can cry together."

Nancy cried because she loved Wanda and hated to see the girl in trouble. Mostly she did not want to see Wanda looked down upon. Tinette had been valedictorian of her class, and Franklin of his. Sara had made almost all A's. Ted had been content to graduate with no grade distinction, but he had been selected as the student with the best character and personality.

Sara and Franklin were upset mainly because of the blight it would cast on the Norris name. "What will people think of us?" had been their theme, accent on the word us. Ted was shaken because he felt responsible for the family, felt that if Grandfather had still been alive, the difficulty never would have developed. Also he wondered if such an action would affect Marguerite. Could Wanda's defiance become a precedent?

Priscilla felt sorry for Wanda. Somehow the girl was misguided, but the scope of it was beyond Priscilla. She had been an excellent scholar with schoolwork, but felt lost in this situation. She could not think how to help, did not know what words to use, if any, and was unable to understand how such a thing could happen in the first place. The look of sympathy on her face went unnoticed by the culprit, who told herself, "Wanda, you are alone against the world."

As for Earl, he felt a smug satisfaction, realizing that Wanda's rebellion took attention away from his recent farce. Actually he never voiced appprobation to his youngest child or even a word of understanding, but when he managed to catch her eye once, he winked in return. Also the day he received his manuscript back from the publisher, rejected by the editor, was the day that interest in any family member expired.

The blow was received hardest by Wanda's mother.

What was Wanda doing to herself, Tinette asked over and over. Where had this spiteful and stubborn streak come from? No thinking of possible answers brought a satisfactory response. Again and again the woman's mind would bring her back to the same puzzle: What did I do wrong? How did I fail Wanda?

Every member of the family saw Tinette's grief and marveled that Wanda could ignore it. Did it not touch her heart at all to realize the terrible despair she had caused her mother? Could she not sense the enormous burden she had placed upon Tinette? Were not the woman's swollen and reddened eyes enough to give Wanda a change of heart? Apparently not.

The family discussed at length what to do about attending commencement exercises. Friends of Wanda, children of the Norris family's close friends, were graduating. Would not their absence show total lack of respect for the graduates and their families? What about the faculty and administrators, many of whom were friends in various social groups and most being regular customers at the store?

Finally, it was decided that Sara and Franklin would attend, and Franklin further decided that Maxine Holz should go with them. It was common knowledge now that there was serious attachment there, and that Maxine was going to write to a certain New York address about business possiblities in that city.

Graduation passed. Tinette's spirit rose to the challenge of what to do about Wanda.

"I shall tell you what I'm going to do," she said at supper one night. "I am going to Manhattan tomorrow."

"To Manhattan? Why?"

"I am going to the college and I am going to throw myself at the mercy of the president there to see what can be done about Wanda's diploma."

"Why, Mother, I don't believe the college can help us in this particular situation," Ted told her.

"Mom," said Franklin, "it is a good idea, but the entrance officer will be the one to see."

"I think it's called matriculatior, Mother," Sara said, "someone in charge of what they call matriculation."

"What can they possibly do in Wanda's case?"

"Ted, that is what I shall find out. She may have to stay there all summer."

"You wouldn't leave her there all alone, would you?" asked Franklin, and Sara followed with, "Without us?"

"We shall have to wait and see what the gentleman at the college tells us. If she has to stay, she'll stay. She has to have her diploma, and we shall have to trust her."

"Shall I drive you over tomorrow, Mom?"

"No. I want Priscilla to take me. And as we return I want her to begin teaching me to drive."

"You?"

"No!"

"Why?"

Marguerite leaned over and patted her grandmother's arm and said, "Please, may I go along? I want to see you drive." Almost everyone smiled at her remark and Tinette gave the child a consenting nod.

Wanda pushed her chair back, rose and stomped out of the room. She had sat through the entire discussion in complete silence.

The registrar at Manhattan gave Tinette hope. Soon records had been obtained from Waterville High and Wanda was enrolled as a student in a special course on the college campus. The course was designed to embrace the last year of high school curriculum plus an introductory college level class. Wanda was duly installed, complete with specific instructions about her behavior. Every Friday she was brought home by her mother in Ted's old

Chevrolet. Tinette had been almost an instant learner behind the wheel, but no more adept at driving than at checking on her daughter.

For a while, Wanda was under several thumbs, strict attention to grades and behavior being given by family and faculty. Surveillance gradually relaxed throughout the following year and Wanda's self began to reappear. She kept it down the first year, but during her second year at school she began to kick up her heels in true Wanda fashion. Literally. She attended every dance on campus and allowed herself to be squired by many a young man both near and far. Before the second year ended she had a reputation for being "fast," and the Dean of Women was relieved when Wanda Norris did not choose to return to Manhattan in the fall.

In Waterville Wanda got a job with Mr. Wilson at the printing office. Maxine Holz had secured the position for her and taught her the ropes. Wanda was only to work mornings until Maxine became Mrs. Franklin Norris, in perhaps another year or so, at which time the newlyweds would take up a new life in New York.

Life was dull in Waterville for the returned co-ed. Her friends either had married or were away at college. She had two boyfriends, neither of whom appealed to short-skirted, short-haired, flapperish Wanda. Caleb Lange farmed up near Hanover and had known Wanda previously. He was one of the brash fellows who liked to hold her tightly as they danced and fling her around in fancy steps that flared out her skirt to show her shapely legs.

The other occasional date came from a slightly older townsman, Curtis Weiss, who owned a small cafe in Waterville. Shyness had always kept Curt from showing an active interest in girls, but he had been introduced to Wanda Norris by her brother Franklin. Franklin and Curtis had graduated from high school together and both had gone to work in their hometown. The cafe where Curt worked, and which he later purchased, was across the street from the general store now called "Norris and Frye." The two boys had done well, and quickly.

Before the end of Wanda's second year at Manhattan, she had practically run one morning all the way into town. It was Saturday, and Franklin had promised to let her have some new dresses. As a rule she wore clothes that were made by her mother and the thought of "store-bought" dresses strongly appealed to her.

By way of showing his appreciation for her going to school (her being away from home was what really pleased him the most), Franklin let his sister select several outfits. Then he took her to lunch at Curt's cafe.

"Eat with us, Curt," Franklin called out to his friend. "You know Wanda here."

Curtis Weiss, properly named since his hair was light blond, as fair as Wanda's was dark black, acknowledged the girl by a formal nod. All three ordered the catfish special, and Franklin told Curt, unnecessarily since it was common talk in town, that the youngest of the Norris family was "learning over at Manhattan."

Being so elated over Franklin's splurge that morning, Wanda beamed upon Curt, shed so lustrous a light upon him, via twinkling blue eyes and toothy smile, that the shy man felt strangely emboldened. While the iron was hot, he struck.

"Nita Naldi is in a movie over at Berner's theater tonight," Curt spoke in a voice he had never even heard before. It was a fairly stong voice and it surprised him. Going for even more volume, he blurted out, "Oh — ah — would you let me take both of us to see it tonight?"

The question as it was worded was so funny to Wanda that she had to put down her fork, and leaned slightly over her plate to laugh. He thought, "I'm sunk," but he was pleasantly surprised when the lovely girl looked up with a laugh still on her lips and told him, "You bet."

As summer came and progressed, Wanda shrugged her shoulders about both beaus. She had a livelier, much more exciting time when she went to dances with Caleb Lange, but those occasions also carried with them huge recriminations after each one. Hanover people had no scruples about tattling to one or another member of the family about Wanda's dancing, her flirting, her gum-chewing, or her choice of companion.

But Curtis Weiss was so utterly mild in his courtship that Wanda nearly scratched him off her list. What held her to him at all was his light blue Nash. Also, she did admit to herself that Curt was so decent. It went farther than his politeness and his respectful behavior. Curt was the same to everyone, child to ancient one. Each time she tried to put a name to his essential quality, it always came out as decency. "And that," she once said to herself, "that is some accomplishment."

Before Maxine and Franklin had married and left town, and while Wanda was still working only mornings, she met a new fellow. Loy O'Neil, only nineteen years old, had moved onto the Walton place. The last renter had left the ground in fair shape, but the shack was disreputable.

The Norris family was agog with excitement. An O'Neil in town! Tinette went to meet him, as per her secret promise to his late father, and was able to contain her resentment. He was alone in the world and bewildered at the task before him. Ted responded to the boy, and after establishing the fact that his father had told of kinship with Calvin O'Neil, although just a distant relationship, he began to instruct the boy in farm work. He lent machinery and tools, he took Loy with him to buy chickens and grain, and was able to report at home that "The O'Neil boy is a natural farmer. Like me," he added with an arch grin.

Nancy told Ted to ask the boy to Sunday dinner. Loy looked nothing like the O'Neils, not a one of them. He was tall and lanky with an easy gait that gave him the appearance of being completely relaxed. He had brown hair with sort of a red tinge to it, not auburn as Tinette's had been, but definitely showing bright red highlights in the sun. He had pleasant gray eyes. His nose looked like the nose of a Shawnee, and old Nancy jokingly referred to him as "Red Thunder."

The family member he liked best was nine-year-old Marguerite, and before too long she was the one who liked him best. Priscilla still insisted on long braids for the child's straight black hair, and Loy liked to play with them, swinging them about as he would pass her.

Immediately after Wanda's discovery of Loy O'Neil, and even after Franklin and Maxine had gone as honeymooners to establish a clothing store in New York City, she took to stopping at the old Walton shack. People soon began calling it a scandal and reporting on the same — Wanda Norris, alone day after day with that O'Neil boy. She was twenty-one and should know better.

At first Wanda stopped on her way home at noon, even took to helping Loy fix up a lunch for them. It was she who encouraged him to brace and repair the little house. Even when he had work to do outside, she would stay on and work diligently on the interior of the house. Together they papered the walls and she painted the woodwork alone. After she had begun to work all day at the printing office, she changed her schedule. Then they would often prepare and eat supper together, in the weak glow of a coal oil lamp.

She saw Caleb and Curt less and less. Caleb did not seem to care, but Curt hung around like a wounded child. A time or two Wanda asked him to join her and Loy for supper. He did, and although he was his usual mannerly self, the situation hurt him.

Tinette once cornered her daughter when gossip had come to her ears concerning Wanda's errant ways. She asked, "Just what is your relationship with this Loy O'Neil?"

"He is the brother I never had. And sister, too."

"Wanda!"

"It is true, Mom. Ted is as stiff as old Black Thunder, and Franklin is as goofy as Sara. They are not like kin, they are like a committee."

About this time it became very noticeable that Earl Norris was "bad off." Ever since his return from New York, he had declined. He was morose, had little appetite, and seldom left the house. His condition became quite apparent at the time of Franklin's wedding. Tinette had helped him dress as he made no attempt to help himself. All of his "good" clothes hung loosely on him. They made him look seedy, but mostly ill.

Sara was all aflutter about her new position in the store, merely a clerk with Franklin gone and Mr. Frye to be the sole owner. Everyone in the family had his own problem to work on, and not much consideration was given to either Earl's illness or Sara's dilemma. Ted and Priscilla were helping Tinette arrange for the new bathroom she was having installed. And carrying it still further, Ted said that a commode and sink should be added as fixtures in one end of the old milk porch.

"It stands to reason that the front bathroom should be used for Grandmother — "

"And for guests," Sara added.

"Yes, for guests." Ted agreed. "So when I or anyone else comes in from outside and needs to wash up — "

"Or use the facility."

"Yes, Grandmother, for any reason, a second commode room will come in handy."

"Splendid idea, Ted — "

"You mean a third such room, Ted," Sara interrupted.

"Splendid," Tinette continued. "And it won't add a whole lot to the other expense."

"Of course, Mother, you realize that this one will come from what Grandfather left me. Right, Priscilla?"

"Right and proper, Ted."

"Well, this is certainly generous of you, Ted."

"It will be a much smaller project than the one you have undertaken, Mother."

"Now," said Nancy. "I shall speak. Last week Flora took me to her cousin Oscar's farm. The floor was warm. The house was all over warm. I want my floors warm. I want the halls to be as warm as the rooms. Ted — "

"Yes, Grandmother?"

"You can just take out those old dirty coal stoves and see about getting a big furnace installed. Today! My treat to the family."

In all of this excitement Earl was nearly forgotten. But for the interest of one person, he might have died in his bed, almost neglected. Wanda observed her father's condition and spoke to Curt Weiss about it. Together they took Earl to Memorial Hospital in Kansas City, Kansas, making a brave effort to save him. But they lost the fight all too quickly because the patient himself had no determination left. Earl Norris was laid to rest in a grave one row to the east of Calvin O'Neil's.

Wanda changed. Before her eyes she had seen a handsome man go down. And it was not a very gradual descent. His flesh began to fall away, as did his hair, his eyes lost life and his hands trembled. Pain jabbed him. At least what Wanda accomplished by taking him to the cancer clinic was to get him some relief from pain. At the last he hardly recognized who she was, but he was not suffering as he left.

Through it all, Curtis had stood by. Not only his large frame imparted strength to Wanda, but his inner presence, too. "How can a man be as good as Curtis Weiss?" she asked herself. Then she asked Curt to marry her, and he accepted, although they both felt that they should wait awhile. The date was set for one year after Earl's death, but when 1929 was nearing 1930, the young couple eloped. Telling no one where they were going, late on Thanksgiving afternoon November 28, they drove in Curtis' light blue Nash to Marysville. There a minister pronounced them "Mr. and Mrs. Curtis Weiss."

CHAPTER SEVEN

Sara

Sara Norris could hardly believe her ears when Franklin disclosed his plan involving Maxine Holz and their idea of going to New York to live. First and foremost she looked upon Franklin as hers. With Ted it was different. He was older and had been interested in Grandfather and the farm work since they were pre-teens. The three of them still had been an entity, but Ted had pursued other interests. Being with Grandfather had meant work, and Ted seemed not to resent that in the least. As a matter of fact, it was clear that he actually welcomed it. She could recall seeing twelve-year-old Ted reach for his mackinaw and cap, put on heavy rubber boots, and with a pleased grin set out with his grandfather for heavy work. Milking, slopping the pigs, currying the horses, cleaning out the chicken house, carrying water, emptying and refilling the tank — any chore that needed to be done.

But Franklin and she had not entered into work around the house or farm to any great extent, just enough to earn their salt, as it was said. Actually just enough to keep their elders off their backs and give them time for their lessons. Before they were out of high school they were already working at Logback's grocery on Saturdays as well as the summer preceding their senior year.

It had been a wonderful opportunity when Franklin had gone in with Arlo Frye to run the general store. The right front side of the store, on the corner, was given over to general soft-goods merchandise. To the left and running parallel to it was a section that held dry goods and children's apparel. That was Sara's domain. Across the back was the grocery store and above it was ready-to-wear for men and women. A sort of balcony that ran the store length was used for shoes. This was a business to be proud of, and Norris and Frye prospered.

But, quite illogically, Sara had always thought of "Norris" as meaning "Franklin and Sara." But the money for it had been lent to and paid back by Franklin; the buying and pricing had been the realm of Franklin and Arlo. Sara's part had been to clerk. Mostly she was sole clerk in the two front sections, but on Saturdays Mrs. Frye came in to help.

It was clearly Franklin's enterprise, and other than Maxine, his only consultant had been his mother. After his trip to New York, he could not rest until he had sold his interest in the store with hopes of securing a place in the Big Life. Tinette understood.

"Each person must live his own life, Franklin. Of course, the hole you would leave here would hurt worse than any cavity in a tooth."

"Mom, don't think that I would enjoy parting from my family. You especially. Don't I know what a rock you are? No other mother anywhere compares with you. But this has to do with the pulse of my life."

"I have every confidence that you will be a success, too. And Maxine is the exact type to respond to it as an opportunity."

This was definitely not the view taken by Sara. In the first place, the death of Calvin O'Neil had jangled her nerves in a way that was hard for her, and everyone, to define. She wept, sobbed, cried and sniffled, privately and with others. But where Franklin's grief had settled down to a solemn acceptance, and where Ted and Priscilla had enfolded their grief to themselves to reside in their hearts as long as they had breath, and where Nancy felt cut in half but told herself to live cut, Sara's manifestation of grief had changed from crying to laughing. She had become a nervous giggler, a puzzle to everyone.

In the second place, Sara had always looked upon herself as Franklin's partner. True, she had rarely been consulted on innovations, but she had been the first to hear of them. In many an instance, an hour or two before closing time, Norris and Frye had held a conference on certain commitments, and always Franklin had disclosed the results to her as they rode home together.

In the third place, she had not been alerted to, and was not aware of the change that had taken place in her brother's recent planning. The news had bowled her over. The three-part news had overwhelmed her: Frye was buying him out, he and Maxine were to be married, and he was leaving for New York with his bride. All imminent, actually, immediately.

Sara reasoned that Maxine Holz was the culprit. She was a girl too young for Franklin, more Wanda's age. Yes, and that provoked her, too. Wanda was positively going overboard to be nice to Maxine. She had heard them laughing together in a way that no girl in her life, particularly Wanda, had ever laughed with her. Too chummy, those girls, and Franklin looking as pleased as punch. He who so often had been irked by Wanda's giddiness.

Everything made Sara either giggle or frown. It made her tee-hee foolishly when she saw her mother practically having to dress Earl Norris. His weakness was actually not at all funny to Sara, but on the other hand she felt little compassion.

The wedding was to be held at St. Mark's, and Ted, who had purchased Franklin's dark blue Buick, was taking the bride and groom to the church and after the reception to the depot. Priscilla said that she would drive the rest of the family down in the old Chevrolet. Flora Stanton was ready to go and was to ride with her husband, Jim, but at the last moment had run across the road to see about a roast she was cooking for supper.

Sara never saw Flora on Sundays, and for this reason had never seen the emerald brooch on her neighbor's breast. On this day Flora was wearing a very pale green voile dress, and the pin shone out handsomely against it.

Sara gasped and although she could see it very well, she stepped closed to Flora and squinted her eyes as if she could barely glimpse the brooch. She giggled nervously.

"Did Grandmother let you wear her brooch today, Flora?"

Flora was in a hurry as Jim was waiting for her, and neither wanted to be late for the wedding. She brushed by Sara and stepped to the other side of the kitchen to let a little water run over her fingers where she had carelessly touched the roast.

"She gave it to me," she said.

Sara quit giggling and went over to the sink. Audaciously and without precedent, she grabbed Flora's arm and whirled her around until they were facing each other. Water splattered onto Sara's fine gray chiffon dress, but she stared at the pin, the stain unnoticed.

"Liar," she said, "that pin is to go to my mother, and as I am the oldest Norris daughter, my mother will — "

Flora tried at this point to pass by Sara. She had never seen such an exhibition and certainly not in the house of Tinette Norris. She felt a bit frightened. Once more the irate Sara grabbed at Flora with her left hand. She missed contact but at practically the same moment her right hand landed a slap on Flora's face.

Instantly, Sara felt a similar blow on her face, and in a

flash realized that Flora had run outside. Sara Norris, prim old maid, stood as if paralyzed. She heard Priscilla honk the horn and she unfroze. On the milk porch was a mirror and Sara practically flew out to look at her cheek. The horn honked again. Then the startled woman glanced down at her dress. On the front above the waist was a wide circle stain where the water had hit the chiffon. It was high enough to be in sharp evidence.

"Sara!" Wanda was at the door calling. "Are you coming?"

"No."

"Why?" Wanda asked as she entered the milk porch.

"Look at my dress. I can't go. Look what Flora Stanton did to my dress."

Even for Wanda's careless ways the dress was water marked too much to wear under ordinary circumstances. Glancing up at Sara's face she saw the red mark.

"Did Flora do that, too?"

Sara's hand went up to her face and embarrassment filled her.

"Get out!" she yelled.

"Sara," said Wanda, "This is August 7, 1929, Franklin's wedding day. It will never come again. He will look for you above all the rest of us. Don't let Flora Stanton spoil that."

Wanda reached out her hand to pull Sara outside and Sara yielded. Thus, she attended the wedding and reception, and she had the satisfaction of being sought out and hugged tightly by the groom before he said goodbye. Although she did feel shame at her behavior, she mostly felt hard rancor against her family. That pin should have been hers. The store should have been hers. By some hook or crook the family should have pulled together in her behalf when Franklin had failed her. These were the thoughts in Sara Norris's mind.

The very next day a traveling minister came to town. The tent where he was to preach was being installed as the Norris sisters walked to work. Sara had to go to work at the store as usual and Wanda was to be full-time worker at the printing office, having taken over the job that Maxine had held.

"Humph" summarized Sara's feeling on that. Sara's thoughts were really centered on her own plight. Now that the Fryes were sole owners of the store, no doubt Mrs. Frye would want to take over her job. And even if she didn't, Sara felt that life might become unbearable with Mrs. Frye "on" her all the time.

The truth was that it was Sara whose personality became unbearable at times. Her brother had been prime owner of the store for so long (actually in Sara's mind it had always been "Franklin's and my store") and now that he was gone, who would defend her? What would happen when with her bossy nature for "taking over," she would insist upon having a sale of certain fabrics that had long been on the shelf? Now what would happen when she left Mrs. Frye alone on the job so that she could take a stroll down Commercial Street, maybe to mail a letter or maybe to go over to the cafe for a dish of ice cream?

No doubt about it, Sara felt miserable. Going into the store as a mere clerk, taking orders from Mrs. Frye, and with no Franklin to whom she could run. "I hate it," she said as she stepped inside the place of doom.

Two big surprises awaited Sara Norris. One was that Mrs. Frye did not appear (this was as it had been for years because Mrs. Frye had followed the pattern of working only on Saturdays). The other was that a man came in early to buy some heavy material, suitable for a drape of some kind. This was Guy Fade, the traveling preacher.

The preacher was not as handsome as he was debonair. From the moment he walked into the store, he assumed an air that seemed to entitle him to the clerk's subservience. Guy ordered, Sara obeyed. Guy soared, Sara bowed. Guy emoted, Sara felt faint. Guy secreted an oily charm, Sara succumbed.

Every day that week through Thursday, Guy and Sara ate lunch together. Guy boasted and bragged, Sara simpered. On the second day and the succeeding one, Sara rushed from her store duty to the tent grounds to be with Guy. She told Tinette she was assisting in the services by stacking the paper fans and laying out the little song booklets, but such was not the case. There was a man and wife team on hand who took care of every single thing that would have been in Sara's province, and the material that Guy had bought on the first day was his last purchase.

On Thursday the Norris family, nearly all of them, went to a carnival in the nearby town of Barnes. Even Curtis Weiss went along to walk over the grounds with Wanda. It was presumed that Sara was at work, but the family had not received word that not only was she not at work, but neither had she appeared at all that day. Not one of the family knew that Sara had spent the morning elsewhere until a very irate spouse told what had happened (also some things that actually had not happened).

About four o'clock the family of eleven-year-old Marguerite Norris had gathered around the Ferris wheel to watch Ted take her on her first such ride. As they made their first complete round, she waved imperiously yet smilingly to her loved ones, especially to Loy O'Neil who had come to stand somewhat behind the family. Considering that one ackowledgment was enough, from then on she concentrated on holding the safety bar and her breath. Once or twice she let her eyes glance up to catch another glimpse of Loy. But her head was down and not even he caught those fleeting glances.

Tinette Norris was actually very beautiful that afternoon. The smile on her face as she watched her darling granddaughter was entrancing. Her blue eyes shone with adoring radiance. White hair with just enough auburn left over the ears and in the Figure Eight knot on top of her head to give color, skin as clear and as unwrinkled as Marguerite's. But not one soul to notice, to feel his breath quicken, to want to push closer to her. Tinette was virtually alone. Of course, there was a woman at home who adored her unequivocally, and Ted readily acknowledged his love for her, but for anyone to be touched by her beauty — She was alone, though not lonely as yet.

As the big wheel made its last round and the family was ready to retrieve Ted and Marguerite, Tinette heard someone in the crowd behind her say, "Look over there. That's the tent preacher and Sara Norris hanging onto him."

It really was. He had his arm around her and was whispering something right into her face. Sara's face was red but it had the silliest expression on it. The woman was simpering and the sight of it sickened her mother. Tinette could not keep the sight away from the family and they were frankly embarrassed. Ted told them to go to the car, that he would get Sara. It took about one minute for the preacher to excuse himself and disappear, and no longer for Ted to lead the shocked Sara to the car.

Arriving home, Sara went straight to the bedroom she shared with Wanda, asking her sister to let her be alone for awhile. As she undressed, she shook. Hardly realizing what she was doing, she donned her nightgown. Meeting Priscilla in the hall on her way back from the bathroom, she tried to pass by silently. But her sister-in-law questioned her as to wanting supper, to which Sara did say, "Oh no. Nothing." She laid on her bed with the sheet pulled up over her legs and tried to think through what this week had brought to her, done to her, what it meant. Instead, she fell instantly asleep.

Early Friday morning, Tinette received two phone calls. One was from Mr. Arlo Frye saying that Sara should not come in unless she was ready to explain the events of the past few days to Mrs. Frye.

"Wait, Sara. That was Arlo on the phone and from the way he talked, maybe you'd better not go down today."

Sara moaned and sank back into her chair at the kitchen table. The phone rang. She heard her mother answer, then give several "Yes," "I see" and "Certainly" responses. Tinette hung up the receiver and all but fainted back into her chair.

"What is it, Mom?" asked Ted.

"It was a woman evangelist, she said."

Sara turned white as a sheet and Priscilla asked if it was the one who was advertised to sing and preach the last two nights of the meeting.

"The same."

"Well, Mom?"

"She is coming out here. Now."

"Why, for evermore!" Ted's voice displayed definite irritation.

"I am going to my room," Sara said as she stood and meekly left the kitchen.

"Yes," Tinette was speaking faintly. "Everyone must get somewhere. I need to see her alone."

Ted stood up and hoisted his jeans in a masterly fashion. He touched Priscilla on the arm and told her to go upstairs and stay with Marguerite, who was still asleep. Then, motioning to Wanda, he bade her be on her way.

"As for me," he said, "if this has anything to do with that Guy Fade and poor old Sara, my place is to be with you, Mother."

The brash and brazen "Brother Guy Fade" drove the

lady evangelist out to the farm himself. Driving completely into the barn lot, he turned his flivver around in a huge circle, then picked up speed before abruptly stopping in front of the house.

With no assistance from the "cloth," the woman got out of the car and walked to the front door. Ted and Tinette welcomed her, albeit stiffly, and asked her to be seated with them in the parlor.

She was stern, an unbending woman one would judge to be over forty years of age. Her large frame was well proportioned and devoid of any fat. She was dressed as suited her "calling," wearing a plain dark dress much longer than the accepted style. Around her throat was a tight white collar, around her head a scarf which hung to her shoulders.

As she spoke she startled both Ted and his mother, filling them with a shameful humiliation. In a low, cultured and rich voice the evangelist (she had introduced herself as "Sister") let Tinette know that her daughter Sara had been very unwise in her actions with Brother Fade.

"Brother Fade is a man who looks at himself as he does his work: here today, gone tomorrow, never to return."

"But Sara — she helped out at the tent — "

"I found them together yesterday morning when I arrived to take up my work at the meeting."

"Together? Do I understand you to be saying — ?"

"Yes, Mrs. Norris. In the tent t-o-g-e-t-h-e-r. And a confession from Brother Fade told me that they had been experiencing such pleasures before. Your daugher was like many other girls and er — uh — older women, in that she believed the line given out by him, the manner which he is wont to speak. I revealed the truth to her, but somehow she was unbelieving and still willing to see him again."

"The truth?"

"Brother Fade is my husband."

Her eyes blazed as she rose to her bony height to bid her hosts goodbye. Tinette sat with her left elbow on the arm of her big chair, her hand covering her face. Ted showed their guest to the door, but not before she had whispered two words to his mother, two words of regret that did not seem too sincere.

"So sorry," she said as she walked out of their lives.

She was gone. The horrible Guy Fade was gone. The revival tent was gone. And with all of it went Sara's self-respect. She could barely make herself take meals with the family. All activity for the pitiful woman stopped as she refused to leave the place.

In Tinette's truthful way, she had revealed the story to Nancy, but once it was told it was never referred to again. Ted told Priscilla, whose empathetic nature led her to tears, but they, too, never mentioned it again. No one told Wanda but in town she picked up enough gossip to piece the saga together.

Sara was ashamed, crushed. She sat in figurative sack cloth and ashes for weeks. "Even Wanda," she said to herself, "even she had enough decency to escape from her wildness and wait for a man she could marry."

The sad, almost unbelievable part of the entire episode was that nothing had happened. Nothing that could be an unremovable blight on Sara's character. The evangelist had entered the tent on that fateful morning to find Sara in Guy Fade's arms! The evangelist's temper blew full blast as she castigated and ousted poor Sara. Sara had then gone to a remote corner of the grounds to wait for the promised excursion in Guy's flivver.

In order to inflame his wife to further heights, the caddish Guy Fade told her that for several days he and Sara had lived intimately in the tent. It was not true.

Sara, in all her innocence, had been filled with the shame merely because she had gone to Guy's tent two nights before the service. That last morning Sara had believed herself to be falling in love. No man had ever shown her such gallant attention before. Her heart was beating in a unusual manner, her stomach had a butterfly or two, and she did not think she could stand to look at yard goods that day. So she had walked around, even into the cemetery, and finally had gone to the tent of her new love. The manner in which he embraced her was shocking to her, not appealing at all. But before she could free herself, they had been discovered.

This innocent behavior had become Sara's shame. Had she talked to her mother about it, or had Tinette questioned her concerning the extent of the brief courtship, Sara Norris might never have left the home of her birth, pride, and rightful place. One thing that worried her a great deal was the advent of Wanda's marriage to Curtis. No definite date had been set, but Sara knew it was bound to be soon. It was an event that she could not bear to witness.

But it was Wanda, after all, who saved her. Phoning home one day from the *Telegraph* Printing Office, Wanda told her mother that an ad had come in for a clerkship in a newly-opened department store in Atchison.

"Mom, try to get Sara to see about it," she urged. "Will you?"

"Well, I don't know. Atchison is a long way off."

"A hundred miles! Go tell her, Mom. I'll wait."

When Tinette returned to the phone, she said that Sara did not to hear about it, nor about anything anyone wanted to tell her.

Wanda sighed and hung up, but when she returned home from work she broached the subject herself.

"Sara. Listen. You know what a first rate clerk you are. There isn't anyone who could handle dry goods in a big city store the way you could."

The girl's enthusiasm sparked an interest in Sara, who finally said that she might answer the ad.

"Oh, no," Wanda told her. "Tomorrow we shall get in Curtis' Nash and we shall drive to Atchison and pick up the job before the ad can even be printed."

And that is the way by which Sara Norris became a clerk, a supervisor, and in time an assistant buyer for a certain department store in Atchison, Kansas. She regained her self-respect, but not until her marriage in 1934 did her family correct their impression of the shame she bore.

Sara had met a widowed gentleman in Atchison, a Dr. Manfried Hammer. He was twenty years her senior and took immediately to her rather old-fashioned ways. They had met quite inadvertently at a concert. Each had attended alone, found themselves seatmates, and had stood for an intermission break together. They met often, not by chance after that, but by mutual agreement. Courtship led to marriage.

When Tinette, Wanda, and Priscilla went into the church lounge after the reception to help Sara dress for the honeymoon trip, Sara was nervously excited. So excited that she hardly knew what she was saying, and she confessed to a terrible fright and fear.

She said, "I cannot imagine what a man — you know, a man and all — is really like. I fear that it will be far different from a kiss."

The realization of what Sara had admitted came to the women, of course, and Tinette cried from relief. She hugged her daughter, and the other women tried to console Sara and calm her fears, and even got her to laughing. The honeymoon must have been a success because the marriage certainly was!

CHAPTER EIGHT

Marguerite

Marguerite Norris loved to sing, and had begun to do so almost as soon as she had been able to speak in conversations. One of her first sentences had been "Hear the little birdie." Her parents were sitting with her in the yard swing when a cardinal flew from the top of the pine tree to a corner of the house. Stopping only long enough to call out his one high note and three lower ones, the red top-knot took his leave.

"Did you hear what she said?" Priscilla asked her husband.

"Yes. She likes the bird, I guess."

"But I mean what she said. A whole sentence."

"Well, I guess that's right." Ted took his little girl onto his lap and hugged her to him. "Say that again, Baby. Tell Daddy what the birdie was doing."

But for the moment Marguerite was not interested in saying sentences. Instead she pointed at where she had last seen the bird, and phenomenally pitched her voice to hum the exact tone of the cardinal, his first high tone. The phenomenon went unnoticed.

In a day or two, the child began to converse. Being fall, daylight was slower in coming each day. At Ted's insistence (his wife hated get-up time) Priscilla was already up and downstairs, yawning in the kitchen. Actually there was no reason for her to be up so early, as Ted's mother was an early riser by nature and always had the breakfast chores in hand. But Ted Norris had been born with the same eyes as his mother, the kind of eyes that snap open even before dawn can have a chance at reveille. And somehow he felt that his wife would tarnish her golden image if she slept while others were astir.

Somewhere Ted had read, "Life is beautiful, but people would rather sleep than look at it." That saying impressed the early-rising farmer, probably because it fit his nature and required no discipline to handle it. Franklin and Sara, like their father, had to be awakened every, every, every, day. This had annoyed Ted all through their school years, and he did not want to be embarrassed by having a wife of that nature.

And so the sweetly compliant Priscilla was yawning in the kitchen when her two-year-old child appeared at the door.

"Marguerite! What is the matter? Couldn't you sleep?"

"I wake."

"And came all the way down those stairs with no light?"

"I came."

By this time, the child's grandmother had picked her up and was nuzzling her.

"Grandmother's darling girl," she said.

"Grandmother," Marguerite said in three distinct syllables.

"Priscilla, did you notice that this little girl held a conversation just now?"

"She did?"

"Yes! You asked her why she was up and she told you. Even told you in effect that the dark had not bothered her. That is smart, Priscilla."

Priscilla was impressed, and when her husband came in from an outdoor chore or two, she bragged to him about it. Everyone heard about it then, but soon forgot because it became a regular occurrence for Marguerite to speak in conversations.

The occurrence that did not receive such a flurry of excitement was the child's singing. The O'Neil-Norris family thought little about music. It was Priscilla who had brought into the family their only real experience with music. Of course, Wanda responded to music in her ability to dance exceptionally well. Priscilla, too, loved to dance, but only with her husband or brothers, and not so frequently as her sister-in-law.

But Priscilla sang a good deal. As she went about the house and yard at one task or another, she sang. Maybe a snatch of a song that her own mother loved, "Silver Threads Among the Gold," or a bit of a song that had been popular during the war, "There's a Long, Long Trail a-Winding."

Marguerite tagged Priscilla a good deal, and one day her short, plump legs were trying to keep pace with her mother's hurried steps as the two of them crossed the side yard. Presently they stopped while Priscilla leaned over to pick up some chicken feathers. The feathers were from the Spanish chicken strain that Grandfather O'Neil had recently introduced to the farm, and the darkness of them shone out in blue and green as they were caught by the sun. Priscilla turned them this way and that to catch the gleam and suddenly she heard the little child sing.

"Over there, over there." Right on pitch, each interval clear.

From then on Priscilla began fostering the talent. The first song she taught the child became a real favorite:
"A birdie with a yellow bill
Hopped upon a window sill
Cocked his shining eye and said,
'Ain't you 'shamed, you sleepy head?' "

The words of the often-sung song endeared the child's ability to Ted Norris and neither he nor other members of the family could hear it enough. Tinette would have been happier had Priscilla not introduced the word "ain't" into Marguerite's ken, but the essence of Priscilla's nature was so naturally pure and sweet that not one of the family ever corrected or criticized her or anything. Not even Sara, who had to stifle jealousy in order to treat her sister-in-law as she deserved. Of course, Ted spoke to her as he liked, but she could handle it.

The advent of the Big War had put a damper on the use of the German language. No more um-pah bands, no German classes in schools, no "Saengervereins." But Priscilla could not let it go entirely, and sometimes when she would rock her child or lie in bed with her, she would softly sing German lieder. One song she sang more than others, until little Marguerite Norris could sing it herself:

"Du, du liegst mir im Herzen
Du, du liegst mir im Sinn.
Du, du liegst mir viel Schmerzen,
Weiss ich wie gut Ich dir bin."

If any of the family happened to be near when she was singing, one or another would join in on the next line:

"Ja, ja, ja, ja. Weiss nicht wie gut Ich dir bin," Marguerite would finish with a little curtsy.

So Priscilla knew that her daughter could sing well, sweetly and accurately, but how unusual was that? Nearly every person in the Katchall family could sing. Also, no attention at all was paid to it by the Norris family who took Marguerite's singing talent more or less for granted, pleasant though it was. Tinette always seemed to respond more to the words than to the tune, and certainly more than to the voice that sang them.

From Sunday School came one song which greatly pleased Tinette. Often she would bid the child to sing it.

"Please go sing that for your great-grandmother," she would say, or "Let me hear our song before you go to bed."

It was a lovely song:

"Let your face with truth be shining
as you pass your neighbor by.
Let your heart brim o'er with music,
like the songbirds of the sky.
Be a merry beam of sunshine.
Be a lily pure and fair.
Be a jewel bright and precious.
Be a blessing everywhere."

This song was just right for "moral" teachings, and Tinette emphasized frequently how much she hoped that it would become a pattern for Marguerite's life. Another of Marguerite's favorite songs had a chorus that kept repeating:

"Daily, hourly be a cheering light.
Glowing, gleaming, beautiful and bright.
Like a beacon glowing in the night,
Glowing gleaming, beautiful and bright."

When she was asked to sing this song at church, the family went to hear her. Ted insisted it was the most beautiful song he had ever heard in church. "A lot better than that slow 'Mighty Fortress' they are always singing."

"Or the 'Church's one foundation,' " Franklin had added.

The family's size had shrunk in quite a hurry, almost all at once, or at least it seemed that way to those who were left. Wanda Weiss now lived with Curtis in the old Pattison house. Tinette had worked for years to keep the sordid facts of Earl's connection there absolutely away from the family and then had all but forgotten it herself. With his death had come an almost unconscious forgiveness on her part for any troubles that Earl and Mary Pattison had brought her. For all practical purposes she

88

forgot, but the odd part of it was that the family didn't. Nancy certainly could not forget. And during certain awakenings that sometimes come during the teen age, Sara had whispered to her brothers all she knew about the situation. They remembered.

The family, all but Wanda, and of course Marguerite, knew. And now Wanda was mistress in the fine old house, now owned outright by her husband. Franklin and his wife were living in New York City in one room behind their store. In letters home they were quite frank to tell about their meager quarters and also very proud to describe the clothing store. So far it was a store exclusively for men's apparel. As it was doing reasonably well, they wrote that they might never change it to include women's dresses and coats, as they had once planned.

Sara, too, was gone from home. She clerked in a department store in Atchison, and from her letters she seemed to be happier than when she had lived at home. Welcoming every new responsibility given to her, she was acquiring an ability that made her more satisfied with herself.

The five who were left at home had varying degrees of nostalgia for times past. Nancy missed them all, but mostly she missed Wanda. Going on ninety years of age, the tiny grandmother had begin to stir about less and less. But every week or two she had Priscilla take her to town. While Priscilla picked up needed items for the table and for the general running of the household, Nancy would stop by to stay with Wanda.

Wanda would serve hot chocolate and maybe a wafer, or as summer progressed, they would drink lemonade. The older woman had two favorite topics of conversation, the enterprising Calvin and the wonderful Tinette. Reminiscing would seem to give renewed vigor to Nancy, and when she was gone Wanda would write it all down.

Ted was surprised at how much he missed Franklin. Since they had been adults, the brothers's work habits had given them little time together, but in their childhood and youth they had been roommates and generally shared life together. It was this earlier period that kept coming to Ted's mind, making him feel Franklin's absence keenly. Priscilla could not miss anyone very much when life was so sweet to her, giving her a loving husband and a precious child. Ted's mother and grandmother were close to her, she having been taught from the time she was a child to respect them. But every once in awhile she thought of Sara, and felt sorry again and again for the embarassment Sara had been made to suffer because of the wretched Guy Fade.

As for Tinette, she took her children growing up all rather philosophically, saying to herself, "They're gone." Seldom did she ever go to visit in Wanda's house, and rare indeed were times when she would ever go to Atchison. Least of all, she missed Earl. After his death, her room took on another change. She sent the twin beds to Wanda and Curt's big house, and once again centered the room around her narrow, cot-size bed. It now had a fine set of innerspring mattresses on it, custom-made, and on it she would stretch out, almost smiling, as if to say, "I'm back. I'm myself again."

Before this last euphoric state came about, however, Tinette cleaned out the desk and shelves, and sent all of Earl's papers and books, even his manuscript, to Maxine Holz Norris, who had offered to work with them in the few spare minutes she had at her disposal. Tinette kept the desk, chair and bookcase because she began to add to her own collection of papers and books. She identified with Dorothy Canfield Fisher, and read and reread whatever books she could find by that author.

Marguerite, like Nancy, missed them all, but never said

a word about it. Her older aunt had never appealed to her, and to a certain extent neither had her uncle. But she was used to seeing them there, and she felt their absence in a wistful way. She was with Wanda a good deal, staying all night at the Weiss home now and then, and going with Wanda to other towns to buy supplies for the cafe. But she still missed Wanda's presence at the farm, and at the table she sometimes thought it had also been nice when her Grandfather Norris had been with them.

But before the "break" in the family had ever occurred, in May of Marguerite's tenth year as she was finishing her fifth-grade work, her parents were called to the school. There was a principal for the entire school, and even a sub-principal who was more or less in charge of the eight grades. But Mr. and Mrs. Ted Norris were summoned to the office of the superintendent himself. They went with considerable trepidation because although the marks on their child's report card were exemplary, her attitude was not. Hardly a day went by that Marguerite did not leave glumly, usually having expressed the wish to her grandmother that she could stay at home. Everyone in the family had learned to dread September because with the fall opening of school would inevitably come tears and sobs from the youngest of the clan. Not that she ever fought or acted out a stubborn refusal, but the sound of those sobs and the pitiful droop of the child's body as she left the house during that first week was an unnerving sight for her elders.

The appointment had been set for four o'clock. Marguerite was to wait in the outer office until the conference had reached a point where she was to be included. At supper that night everything was explained.

"They have put Marguerite in the seventh grade for next year."

"What about sixth grade?"

"They've skipped her?"

"How do they know she is ready for it?"

Ted went on to explain that her fifth grade teachers had gone to the superintendent back in February with the belief that Marguerite Norris could handle sixth grade work right along with her regular assignments. They had asked for permission to try it. As it was an experiment, it was to be done completely in secret, no one was to know about it, not even the child herself.

"Her arithmetic teacher slipped a bunch of sixth grade problems in with her other work, calling her up to the desk for whatever explanation she would need. Her grammar and spelling teacher did the same thing."

"They say there is no story she cannot read and understand, and remember perfectly," bragged Priscilla.

"No word she can't spell," added Ted.

Everyone was proud and also vastly amazed. Tinette, of course, knew how smart she herself had been in school, but as Priscilla told about Marguerite's ability to read and understand what she had read, her mind recalled something else.

"She is like you in that, Earl," she had told her husband. "She has your own ability along that line."

Earl Norris had been shocked to hear himself praised, even given credit for some of his granddaughter's intelligence. He could hardly believe it, nor could he keep a smile from his face. But it was only after many had spoken words that Earl did not even hear that he could frame words to say, "Thank you, Tinette, but the working of your own fine mind is no secret to anyone."

Wanda was the one to sense an underlying truth to the event. "Why, little girl," she said, "the work was not too hard for you. It was boring! You little scamp."

At this point Priscilla could keep still no longer on yet another subject. She told them that the English and arithmetic teachers were not the only ones who had noted special ability in Marguerite.

"The music teacher was there, too, and she says that next fall she intends to start Marguerite on voice lessons."

"How do you mean, voice lessons?" Franklin had asked.

"Dear Brother," Wanda said impatiently, "she means do-mi-sol-do."

"Yes, Franklin, she means that Marguerite's voice is to be trained, 'cultivated,' as she said."

"I am not one bit surprised," said Nancy, peering from the far end of the table to bring the child into focus. "No bird can match you, Honey."

"Oh, Mother," said Tinette, "what a sweet way to say it. I knew this child was unusual. This is the happiest day of my life."

"That is not all," said Priscilla, sitting up straighter now and leaning forward in order to see everyone. "They want us to start her on piano right away."

"Piano?"

"Goodness sakes!"

"Do you want to, Marguerite?"

The child who had sat so still during the recital of her accomplishments now seemed about to cry. She sank back against her chair and placed both hands in her lap.

"With all my heart," she said, and then added, "longingly."

Sara gave a little gasp at the response from Marguerite, then asked, "Will Mrs. Kelley be a good enough teacher to start her?"

Everyone had agreed that as a piano teacher, Mrs. Kelley was widely praised.

Franklin cleared his throat and spoke as if he were giving an oration from a pulpit, "Congratulations, Marguerite. To be diligent in your school work is to be excellent in general. I, myself, was valedictorian of my high school graduating class, as was your grandmother before me. And as Mother pointed out, my own father has always given himself to the reading of books and the gaining of knowledge. Now five years have passed since you have seen your great-grandfather, but Calvin O'Neil was one of the smartest men who ever lived, and our dear grandmother here will attest to that."

"It's the truth, Franklin," Nancy agreed, "but now I am ready for my pie. What kind did you make, Tinette?"

"Butterscotch, Mother, by your same old recipe, and I shall get it right now."

"Hold on!" said Franklin. "Sit back down just a moment, Mom, while I finish. Thank you. What I am going to say now gives me a great deal of pleasure. And here it is: I, myself, am going to buy the piano. I would have it no other way."

Gasps from Sara, smiles from everyone, advice from Ted as to what kind it should be.

"Better make it a secondhand one, Franklin. No one knows if she will even take to it," Ted cautioned.

"Of course she will, Ted," Priscilla told him with not a small hint of annoyance in her voice.

"No, no," Franklin said. "It shall be brand new, and my dear little niece, it shall be yours."

"Hurray!" yelled Wanda.

Marguerite pushed back her chair and went around to her uncle. She kissed him and he pulled her onto his lap, where she sat to eat a large piece of butterscotch pie.

School ended and with it came a written guarantee that Marguerite Norris would begin the fall term, a month before her eleventh birthday, as a seventh grader. Within a couple of weeks, a truck from the Jenkins Music Company of Kansas City, Missouri, drove onto the O'Neil farm carrying a large box.

Ted Norris signed for it and helped the driver with the uncrating of a piano. Its legs lay beside it, making it an easy, though heavy piece of furniture to carry. Because the south wall of the parlor was the place for the piano, some rearrangement of furniture was necessary. It was a Chickering quarter grand, a beautiful piece of furniture with a marvelous resonant tone.

Marguerite had already taken four lessons from Mrs. Kelley so she would be familiar with the keyboard when the piano arrived. She showed the family where "middle C" was located. Then she played every "C" on the piano. Lastly she placed her left little finger on the "C" below "middle C." Then with her right hand placed one octave above "middle C," she played the notes up and back in a capriciously fast run. Applause! Applause!

Marguerite Norris was ten years old all summer, as her birthday was not until nearly a month after school would begin in the fall. But that summer she grew old. Not old-old, but ancient old. Playing the piano came easily to her and she literally lived at the instrument, practicing hours each day and playing mini-concerts for her family each evening. It taught her. She learned about emotions from it. She could enact complete scenarios on the piano, making this phrase jump for joy, and that one weep in grief. Indeed, she played entire lifetimes out in various pieces, or sometimes all within one selection. She drew music from the piano. It drew away her childhood.

All through her life Marguerite would run to the piano to express feelings of ecstasy, feelings of futility, feelings of empathy for various situations that were not even her own. She used the piano to enjoy life, also to cope with it, and in learning to do so, she brought pleasure to many people.

When Marguerite had been playing the piano for over

a year, she lost her most constant listener. Tiny shriveled Nancy O'Neil had kept to her habit of sitting in the parlor, although of late she had needed to be helped across the hall to a chair which she now preferred to the sofa. She never tired of hearing the piano. Sometimes she would express regret that she had never been taught to play herself. She even spoke to Calvin, right out into the air-waves she would say, "We should not have waited so long to get Tinette her piano."

Finally, she began to confuse Tinette with Marguerite, until to the old lady the two actually became one person. Any selection Marguerite played would bring a smile of satisfaction to Nancy's face, but her two most constant requests were "Over the Waves," ("Sobre las Olas," Marguerite liked to call it) and "Robin's Return."

At last Nancy Hawkins O'Neil was unable to go to the parlor or even to leave her bed. She only lasted two days in that state, but Marguerite never left the bedroom during that time. Her mother fixed a reclining chair for her to sleep in, and during the daylight hours she sat close to Nancy's bed. The second night passed and Priscilla had entered the bedroom carrying a tray when all at once the "light" went out. Nancy was gone. She had left holding tight to Marguerite's hand and saying "Tinette."

After this, Marguerite's music took on new depth and she experienced a renewed desire to practice even harder. As the years passed she matured quickly. Even her size exceeded that of the average girl her age. As a senior in high school, the youngest in her class by one full year, she nevertheless was the largest. Not necessarily the tallest, but there was a breadth to her straight back and to her full breast that gave her the appearance of a large girl. Indeed, she remained the same beautifully proportioned size all her life.

Music became nearly everything in Marguerite's life. Her voice matured early into a sweet contralto, greatly in demand for concerts, even for weddings and funerals. At many of the town's music concerts one of the main events would be a piano number by Marguerite Norris. She kept up well with her schoolwork and always reacted kindly to the family's tenderness toward her. But her music came close to being "everything."

Not quite. There was a person whom Marguerite had loved for many years, one who occupied many of her thoughts, one her piano talked to daily. That was Loy O'Neil. In a way, the piano lessons had fanned their friendship, made a keyboard for them to play on.

Whenever Loy had Sunday dinner at the farm, usually every week, he sat across the table from Marguerite, next to Wanda and Curt. He simply could not keep his eyes off the pretty girl with her blue eyes, shining black hair, and velvet white skin. In order to hear her laugh he would tell jokes; in order to see her grin he would find some little thing to tease her about.

But nothing about her intrigued him more than her music. He always thought of it as "Marguerite's wonderful talent of music." When the family left the table, the women to do the cleaning up, the men to stroll outside awhile, Loy could hardly wait until they could all reassemble in the parlor. Then Marguerite would play and sing, and a lump would form in Loy's throat and a joy would fill his heart, and he knew not whether he wanted to cry or to laugh.

During the summer of 1934, before Marguerite's sixteenth birthday, Wanda and Curtis went on a trip to St. Louis. Curtis felt he could not be gone long from his cafe, especially in late July when various harvesting crews were traveling in and around Waterville, but Wanda was eager to try out their new two-tone tan Pontiac. She argued that the Missouri roads were paved and that the car would really "make time." Curtis yielded to her enthusiasm.

Before they left, Wanda had a private talk with Ted and Priscilla.

"Curtis and I are going to drive over to see the beautiful park in St. Louis, and we want to extend the advantage to Marguerite and Loy."

"Why that park? What is in it?"

"A zoo for one thing, but mostly I have read about their gardens. A real tourist attraction."

"I would hate to say no and make the little girl miss the advantage and all, but why Loy?" asked Ted.

"How would you manage at nighttime?" Priscilla added, almost in a whisper.

"We'd get a hotel in Kansas City, and then one in St. Louis. Same way back, stop in Kansas City."

"No, no, I mean, uh — how would you manage?" still whispering.

"Loy could bunk up with Curtis, and I would certainly keep Marguerite in a room with myself."

"What do you think, Ted?" Priscilla asked, now in a normal tone.

Wanda interrupted to say, "It is not as if they haven't started seeing each other. He has been taking her to movies for nearly a year now and you let them go over to Barnes for the carnival together."

"But she is still so young."

"Marguerite is not so young as her age. At times she seems as old as I am."

"Well — "

The arrangement was settled, but the news of it threw Tinette into a dither. Marguerite was too young to go to St. Louis. She would be seeing entirely too much of Loy. It had the appearance of two married couples off on a trip.

So she commented, but to no avail. The trip was made.

"If only Mother were still here. I could ask her what she thought. Maybe she could talk to Marguerite."

The tourists returned within a fews days and all of them gave exciting reports of the sights they had taken in. Then life resumed as usual. Except for Tinette. She felt a strange agitation, as if Weston O'Neil were back to bring grief to Marguerite. Something made her want to get her granddaughter away from this Loy. Not that she disliked him, as there was nothing unfavorable in his makeup.

"Well, he is too old," Tinette told herself. "And Marguerite is too, too young. Not even sixteen. And she has no business being serious about a man who is ten years her senior."

Thus she would speak about the situation, sometimes to Ted or to Priscilla, and sometimes to her mother's empty bed.

"They are too close. Marguerite needs to get away, live somewhere else."

That was an impractical solution, but Tinette found a way to accomplish it briefly anyway. She went on a trip herself, taking Marguerite to Hot Springs, Arkansas. They had never been happier. They reveled in the train ride, complete with berth privileges, they laughed at the rugged steam and ice "baths" at the hotel, they walked over the hills of the town. Tinette even arranged for Marguerite to play and sing in the hotel parlor. Much to the delight of everyone, she was asked to do a repeat performance. The two were like girls together, Tinette forgetting her sixty-plus years, and also forgetting Marguerite's tender age as the girl projected herself so maturely. Later Tinette thought of that and had to admit to herself that Marguerite was hardly the average sixteen-year-old.

The train trip home was splendid, but they neared their destination with different feelings. Tinette felt she was returning to nothing. "Mother is gone," she thought. "Ted and Priscilla are an entity. They don't need me." But the feeling she could not bear to express, even to herself, was a mistaken foresight she had concerning Marguerite. Something seemed to tell her, "This is the last time for Marguerite and me." At last Tinette O'Neil Norris knew what it was to be more than alone. She was lonely.

But expectations were bright inside Marguerite. She not only hoped that Loy would be at the depot waiting for her, she expected it! Stepping off the train behind her grandmother, she kissed her parents and then walked right into the arms of Loy O'Neil. They did not kiss, but their embrace told everyone, especially Wanda, who had run late to the depot, that their fate lay within one another. To Marguerite, this in no way excluded Tinette from her life. She knew that all of her life she would be sharing her ups and downs with the grandmother she loved so much.

During Marguerite's last year of high school, she became really expert in her music. She went to the state contest, representing the district as contralto soloist and as pianist, playing Chopin and singing Oley Speaks' music. She was awarded first place in both. The scholarship she received was for a degree in music from Kansas University in Lawrence.

But Marguerite did not want to be a highly-trained professional, being dragged here and there for one concert followed by another. Her parents had taken her to the contest in Topeka, but Loy had arrived in time to hear her play. Wanda and Curtis were with him, and for the return trip Marguerite rode with them. As they rode she made her position plain to them. She was not going to accept the scholarship.

Later the discussion continued at home. Marguerite's parents both understood what she was saying and agreed with her.

"It's your life, Baby," Ted told her, "and you can spread your joy wherever and however you like."

Strangely enough, Tinette also agreed, with one stipulation: "Just so you get your college work somewhere."

But as high school graduation drew near, the young couple wanted to marry. The idea was presented at the habitual Sunday after-church dinner. Tinette was seated at her usual place with Marguerite beside her. Between Marguerite and her parents sat Loy O'Neil, scrubbed to shining and handsomely clad in a lightweight, tropical wool suit ordered from "Norris Clothier" in New York City. Across from them sat Curtis and Wanda, and Jim and Flora Stanton. At the extreme end, two chairs sat vacant so that everyone could see the photographs of Calvin and Nancy O'Neil.

Flora and Priscilla had taken care of the meal. Everyone was just finishing bowls of delicious strawberry shortcake in cream when Loy cleared his throat.

"If your strawberry shortcake was that delicious last year, Priscilla, I had forgotten it. Thank you for a wonderful meal."

"Oh, now," Priscilla began.

Loy interrupted her by saying, "It was fitting to have this extra surprise today because Marguerite and I have decided to ask permission to be married."

Complete silence. Each spoon was laid down. Every mouth was touched by a napkin. Every eye was on the young couple.

"Well, Ted?" asked Loy as he reached for Marguerite's hand.

"Well, Loy, I don't know what to say. I guess you rightly should ask Priscilla here."

"Well, Priscilla?" the young man asked smiling.

"I — uh Loy, ah — uh Ted," the woman stammered as

she glanced at first one man and then the other. "I guess the right one really to ask is Marguerite herself."

"Oh, thank you, Mother," said Marguerite softly.

"Wait!" Tinette spoke now in obvious agitation. "You have not had proper schooling yet, Marguerite, and to tell you the truth, I think you should have a wider experience of — well, of dating. Maybe meet some boys at college. What do you think, Wanda?"

Wanda thought a moment and then spoke. "Mom, Loy here appreciates Marguerite's talents. He enjoys her music, he loves it. She could go to school somewhere, meet up with some fellow in music school who would spend his life squelching her talent. Be jealous of it."

No one spoke for a moment and then Wanda added, "I really cannot see your point of view, Mom."

"Well I can see yours, Wanda," said Ted. He laid his napkin on the table and said, "Well, Priscilla?"

"Yes, I can see Wanda's point. I understand her idea. What do you think, Flora?"

"I believe they know what they're doing. Do you, Jim?"

"I know little ole Nancy loved this Loy."

"So, then," and Ted was about to rise from the table.

"Wait!" said Tinette. "Marguerite has to have more training. She has to have college work, don't you, Honey?"

"I guess so, Grandmother."

Then followed the real discussion, the actual working out of the details. They talked as they cleared the table, as they carried out the leftovers for the chickens and the pigs, as they cut up the remaining chicken for supper salad, and as they finally regathered in the parlor. They talked together and they talked separately and they talked in groups that kept changing until they were once again one big group in the parlor.

"So, Marguerite," asked Tinette. "Will you then agree to attend music school at Emporia this summer? As we have pointed out, Dr. Beach's music department rivals even those at Lawrence and Pittsburg."

"Yes, Grandmother, I want to with all my heart. But I must be with Loy each and every single weekend."

"Let him come every Friday to bring you home," Ted suggested.

"But if there are weekend concerts that she should attend — " from Tinette.

"Then Loy will just have to stay in Emporia those weekends with me."

"And when that happens, I'll make Curtis here go with me, and we'll come, too," said Wanda. "All right to do that, Marguerite?"

"Yes, of course. But sometimes I would want Grandmother to come along. As a matter of fact, it just came to me, Grandmother. Why don't you come with me and spend the summer there?"

Tinette blushed with happiness and everyone talked at once until Marguerite stood to her feet. Quiet resumed and the girl spoke.

"Our wedding will be postponed then until my seventeenth birthday in September."

To the amazement of the couple, no one demured. Hugs and handshakes followed. Ted even called Loy "Son," and Priscilla began figuring on which bedroom would be theirs. Wanda went back twice to embrace her, and Jim Stanton was thinking, "The O'Neil farm will really be the O'Neil farm again."

Tinette was the first to speak.

"Let's all sit down. I would like to hear Marguerite play 'Robin's Return' and 'Over the Waves.' For Mama."

THE END

Share the Warmth of the Capper Fireside Library!

Other Capper Fireside Library Titles Currently Available:

These Lonesome Hills ◆ Letha Boyer
Home in the Hills ◆ Letha Boyer
Born Tall ◆ Garnet Tien
The Turning Wheel ◆ Garnet Tien
Lizzy Ida's Luxury ◆ Zoe Rexroad
The Farm ◆ LaNelle Dickinson Kearney
The Family ◆ LaNelle Dickinson Kearney

──────────── ◆ ────────────

For more information about Capper Press titles
or to place an order, please call:
(Toll Free) 1-800-777-7171, extension 107,
or (913) 295-1107.

These Lonesome Hills by Letha Boyer

Anne Davis is full of youthful optimism when she leaves St. Louis for the Ozark hills to teach in a one-room, eight grade schoolhouse. Eager to broaden the horizons of her rural students, she finds her efforts thwarted by the overpowering forces of tradition, lack of knowledge, and poverty. How can she gain the support of a hostile community? Will that handsome young man help her or is his interest of a more personal nature? Will Anne follow her heart and find happiness in these lonesome hills?

One of the first four *Capper Fireside Library* novels, **These Lonesome Hills** begins the story of the adventures Anne and Davy have in the Ozark hills, and how they develop a friendship as Anne develops a love for the land and her students. You'll love the tale — **These Lonesome Hills.** *Quality softcover,* **0017, $6.95**

Turn the page for details about the charming sequel to These Lonesome Hills!

Home in the Hills by Letha Boyer
The enchanting sequel to **These Lonesome Hills**

Newlyweds Anne and Davy Hilton begin their
marriage by living with his parents while Davy
builds a home of their own. A teacher at a one-room
schoolhouse, Anne crusades to improve her students'
lives in this poor, Missouri Ozarks community only to
find herself drawn into family dilemmas. How can
she help Calvin, her special student, escape the
clutches of Granny Eldridge? Will her proud but
impoverished neighbor, Jane Decker, accept help?
Can Anne and Davy make a home in the hills?

This delightful sequel to **These Lonesome Hills**
continues Anne and Davy's story, as Anne makes a
lifelong commitment to Davy and her love for the
Ozark mountain country. There are surprises and
shake ups as the saga continues — **Home in the
Hills.** *Quality softcover,* **0006, $6.95**

**Watch in 1992 for Letha Boyer's third Anne
and Davy novel, coming from Capper Press!**

Born Tall by Garnet Tien

Tomboy Lucinda Meek would rather climb fences and run barefoot than be a "little lady." Yet Papa Dryce insists she act "born tall" like a Meek. Her young heart torn between love for her father whose proud, aristocratic ways and ambitions for wealth dominate the family, and for her mother whose simple faith and kind ways give gentle guidance, Lucinda struggles to find answers. Can she step out from the shadow of her father's domination? Can she teach him what it truly means to be born tall?

The second of Garnet Tien's *Capper Fireside Library* novels, **Born Tall** deals with a theme many identify with — a child choosing values for herself from her parents' examples. This is a classic tale of growing up, complete with the confusion and sometimes anger that accompanies new feelings and frustrations. Witness one family's struggle to overcome — **Born Tall.** *Quality softcover,* **0001, $6.95**

The Turning Wheel by Garnet Tien

Casting his fate to the wheel of life, young Brin
Bruner joins Alphabet Cane and his granddaughter
Fay, as they travel by covered wagon to the Ozarks
seeking their fortunes. Brin dreams of wealth, and of
founding a town where families can start life anew
after the Civil War. With unyielding faith, Brin
pursues his vision of placing good deeds on the
turning wheel of life. But dark forces threaten Brin's
dream. Good or evil, what will come round on the
turning wheel?

One of two *Capper Fireside Library* novels by author
Garnet Tien, **The Turning Wheel** is a classic story of a
young man's quest for a dream. But as optimism
meets a dark reality, this young man must make
choices that may change the course of his life. Brin
must make his good deeds outweigh the bad on the
turning wheel of life — **The Turning Wheel.** *Quality
softcover,* **0020, $6.95**

Lizzy Ida's Luxury by Zoe Rexroad

Life is tough when you are 12 years old and your biggest dream is a piano of your own, but your Papa says it's a luxury you can't afford. Lizzy Ida's adventures and the experiences of her family, the McReels, are the backdrop for this heartwarming story of a family surviving the year 1924, and of a little girl working toward a big dream. Despite an eventful year and several setbacks, will Lizzy Ida meet the challenge of getting a luxury of her own? Will the music in her heart be shared?

Lizzy Ida's Luxury, the first of the four new *Capper Fireside Library* titles, was inspired by author Zoe Rexroad's mother, who worked diligently selling newspaper subscriptions to win the grand prize in the sales contest — a piano, and by Zoe's love for music. It is the story of a family surviving on the farm, and enjoying life's little pleasures while striving for their dreams — **Lizzy Ida's Luxury.** *Quality softcover,* **0028, $6.95**

Carpenter's Cabin by Cleoral Lovell

It is often said that opposites attract, and in this contemporary romance with old-fashioned values it certainly seems to hold true. It was love at first sight for an unlikely pair — Holly remodels and Dan writes. Grow with them as they struggle to overcome lifestyle differences and outside hostilities while building their relationship as well as a bridge to Carpenter's Cabin. This story contains all of the elements of a classic: a heady romance, a hidden hideaway, the revenge of a jealous suitor and a stark misunderstanding that threatens a rosy future. Will Dan and Holly write their own happy ending, or is it too late to reconstruct their romance?

This second new novel in the *Capper Fireside Library* series strays from the first five novels, because it is written in a more contemporary setting. It was, however, one of the most popular of the stories serialized first in *Capper's*, hence its entrance into the *Fireside Library*. You will enjoy the refreshing sense of traditional values in a more modern world as much as you have in previous *Fireside Library* titles — **Carpenter's Cabin.** *Quality softcover,* **0029, $6.95**

The Farm by LaNelle Dickinson Kearney

Brought together in a makeshift Union hospital, Calvin O'Neil and Nancy Hawkins pledge their lives to one another, and to making a life on a Kansas homestead. As they embark on their lifelong adventure, they encounter an unlikely Indian ally and struggle against the forces of man and nature, loneliness, and years of failed crops and no money. Isolated from family and friends, they struggle to succeed on the farm while looking to the future. Will their love be enough to carry them through? Can the legacy of the O'Neil farm be saved?

This is the first of LaNelle Dickinson Kearney's novels, the second being **The Family. The Farm** begins the saga of the O'Neil family, and takes you through sixty-three years in Calvin and Nancy's life together. It is a story of heartbreak and disappointment, but also of love, friendship and eventually triumph that will make your own spirit soar. This is the beginning of a broad and strong family tree — **The Farm.** *Quality softcover,* **0030, $6.95**